"EMPTY NEST"

AND OTHER STORIES

Angelyn Spignesi Kopylec Arden

En Route Books and Media, LLC
Saint Louis, MO

Make the time

En Route Books and Media, LLC

5705 Rhodes Avenue

St. Louis, MO 63109

Cover credit: Sebastian Mahfood from author photos

ISBN-13: 978-1-956715-36-1

Library of Congress Control Number: 2022934047

For four decades now, I've been studying, living through, as well as writing on and from what moves between Spirit and Matter: the figures, landscapes, intentions, and language of that "space". Diotima (in Plato) and Simone Weil have called this "metaxy". I have written on the figures and land-scapes of the psyche moving in orbits of symphony: the "space", or, better stated, the communication between Spirit and Matter as a complete interactive circuit. These stories come from there.

I am very thankful to those who were readers of one or more of these stories: Clare Adamo, Ken Kopylec Arden, Caitlin Celella, Susan Croft, Diane Darling, Robert Harrison, Carola Hillman, Marie Hoffman, Susan James, Debra Johnston, Sr. Dolores Liptak, Sebastian Mahfood, Jennifer Ristine, Kathy Senecal, and Jerry Spignesi.

For Kathy Senecal

TABLE OF CONTENTS

Empty Nest 1

The Episode 69

The Forgotten-About Town 113

Sarah and the Idea: A Young Adult Story 145

Mae: A Prose Poem 189

The Night Walk and the Water 217

EMPTY NEST

The lounge chair had plastic strips and where they wore into my skin no longer bothered me. It was the sort of contact I appreciated in fact. The small table nearby had enough of a surface for an iced tea. Yet the small hole in the ground beneath and to the right of it, which I only now had just noticed, was provocative.

Enough of holes wanting! Is it still the time for the lunge, must a hole still be here, where will be the peace? At closer purview, I saw what could be a tiny diving board over the hole. Since I knew I magically had not grown in size over the night, I wondered how a swimming hole so small could be in my vicinity keeping me huge.

Enough on size rumination, just look at the thing. Words coming from a voice of whom was once alive, close to those who know. Bending my shoulders to it, this small hole I call swimming, swimming hole. Bending shoulders and what will fall off will. Hear the clatter. Or I could rub my left jawbone and finish the release of outpourings insured and cleared. Cleared for takeoff, I bend to it and look in.

Sure, a bit of a diving board was there and the little feet that had traversed it hardly left any wet marks. They never asked for much. But who dove in anyway and is there any water here? Looking in could create the image, could it not? Could this image that there should be water, it be a water hole, actually allow and even necessitate my seeing such? Stop, just look. Again, it speaks.

So, I did look, both eyes open. I was not disappointed. Little people swimming with abandon and really looking very happy. I was no Gulliver or Alice, but I did wonder. I don't want to scare you, I said as softly as possible, but how are you? Can you see me? What day is it for you?

A few of them looked up as if a jet plane swiftly had passed by, and, as if they were satisfied in finding its tracks, they went back to their activity. But no one down there registered me. Now three youngsters were climbing onto the diving board. They were giggling. That sort of joy is the music keeping the globe evenly pacing itself daily, I thought. That is the music of every jewelry box holding the jewels of this life. One by one they ran full speed to the end of the board and jumped off. Not one belly flop in the three jumps, more like knives were entering the water. They swam together, dog paddling as they spoke and then they laughed and spoke some more.

I shifted in the lounge and perhaps woke and there was no swimming hole, no board, nothing but the dank dirt of an area beside this porch. The indentations in my skin from the lounge's plastic strips told me it was time to get up, so I did, feet and legs over one side, flip flops on and standing, breathing getting deeper as I oriented more to this land, this porch, this rest.

While I was entering the kitchen, the plans for the day bellowed at me from the corners, from out of the refrigerator, from the cold hollows of stove and sink. Get supplies. Yet the floor did not mind the dirt, that was one thing of which I was sure, it would let a couple of weeks go by before it would bellow at me.

The swing on the tree outside the house had laughter and so I looked. There is an actual child this time, we had given the neighbors permission contingent on the watchfulness of an adult. And there was his mother sitting by the swing as it entertained them both. Such a simple mechanism for joy. Her presence sitting there compelled me to go out and say hello, to companion, welcome and amuse if necessary. But I went upstairs to change instead. The stripes on my back were there indeed yet fading as surely must be the swimming hole itself.

Where are those children now, I wonder - the ones who spent that day in sun and water shining and rising to both? Are they tucked in bed, are they with pillowed dream and fantasy, are they drifting in the space where I was when I met them?

Their parents would have bathed them, put on pajamas with cartoon figures and large buttons. Their parents may have read the current story or slapped their knees when recounting a joke. It was all the same. No matter the evening ritual, sleep would come, and the children would dream right into the space where I had first met them. Later, as the day progressed, I would say it was a mistake or an error that I thought I had been in such a space with such little, very little people. For these spaces evaporate and in their stead incredulousness mounts not to be denied.

Can I see the engine of your new car? The neighborhood boy came over, the same one who had been on the swing the day before. I opened the hood and the heat emanating from it surprised us both. He knew more about it than I ever would and I looked at him with appreciation for his ability to approach me for this interior view. Afterwards, I walked him back to his home casually chatting. On the way, I surveyed the circular patch of pansies around the oak.

The pansies were doing well despite the lack of rain for days. The oak itself had been my steadfast friend for a long while. It was something about its stature, its unequivocal generosity of spirit, its poise; I took from it and did not offer much back except the simple gesture of the pansies surrounding its base.

Base luck some would say but I knew better. Everything had to be earned, warranted. The time was eleven already. The main tennis matches had been played and won or not on the other side of the world. I had wondered about scores and who really kept such or if it was an issue of numbers and degree. I was past caring about such now.

More errands or should I try to find those little people, the children again? They were a comfort to me now past raising my own and entering the latter phases of life. A bell clanged with mediocre loudness at midnight. Then I knew to look, they were beckoning me? I arranged the bedcovers after getting up, my husband's gentle snores allowed this entry without disturbance.

I went into the other room, the one for hobby, for guests, for storage. I sat in an uncluttered chair and found my new friends quite easily. They were out of the swimming hole and in the surrounding wood now. They were gathering sticks for a fire where they were making a treehouse. Though they were still rather sopping wet, they worked diligently, and the remnant of the pond water cooled their sweat, so it did not annoy them.

For nothing annoyed this group. I saw about five of them. It seemed as though I was no one in their purview and that was fine by me.

Then, as if a switch turned, one began to tell me a story as if he had known me already and even assumed I'd be there. It was a fable about a donkey who did not 'take' the burdens anymore. I assumed there would be a goddess in it, but the boy proceeded in another direction. It was the hooves that mattered here: hooves making marks in the sand so those about to treat a girl as badly as they would a luggage carrier would stop to see the marks.

Some of the children listening to the story remembered the Bible story, others just assumed it was a message to them, private, channeled from the heavens. The marks made geometric designs and they were calming; they had a certain certainty though no one knew exactly what they meant. Donkeys can proceed better this way, the donkey said to anyone who listened.

I stopped the boy here - are you making up the story? I asked. Or is this the one that was handed down to you? It's for you, is all he said, and then he turned and went back to building the fort with his friends.

I turned on the light in the room and lay for a bit on the spare bed. I thought of all the children in the world building forts, perhaps at this very instant, and I thought of all those others who would be enthralled, for whom it would be beyond belief in order to be able to do so. I was beginning to fall asleep, so I went back into the bedroom to be with John.

Time passed and I was forgetting about the children, the swimming hole, the fort and the fable. I was at my desk at work topped with piles of papers necessary and not necessary and my colleague came over again the second time that day. He was young, in his 20's, and full of expectation, a freckled face and reddish hair adding to his bounding energy of hope and guarantee. His pants verged on jeans and his shirt was striped, casual and ironed most likely by someone he knew. It occurred to me that he reminded me of the boy at the fort with the fable, yet grown.

I looked up to him eagerly since it was his demeanor, his overall welcoming of another that warranted such. I took a deep breath to steady myself in the reception of his energy, the flux as well as the delight of it. He was fiddling with a button on his shirt. Out with it lad, I thought. I looked at his eyes. They weren't focused but were charming in the way they transmitted another place, a different space from the one locally in front of us both.

I looked at his right hand which was holding some papers. I took them from him assuming that they contained what were relevant to whatever he was not saying and from wher-ever his eyes had removed themselves. The papers were memos. They were reports on how he had or had not yet met his agenda. Was he asking for advice on how to proceed? I looked at his eyes again, now they actually were looking at me. They seemed more focused as if they had ceased being in that other space and transmitting that and more that they had left that space to be here actually with me. What do you want? I asked him slowly, deliberately.

I want to know how I can finish the template without doing only what others want and with being myself doing it. So that was it, I was one who had not fallen under and had not been molded and had survived. He was recognizing such and, in a way, complimenting it while wanting it for himself.

It's different for each how that can happen, I began in what now, for the first time ever in our work together, was an ex-change. I said to him: It may be easier for you for various reasons. I started to give him my sense of the necessity of de-tachment in the workplace accompanied by total commit-ment to the work itself and those doing the work. Then I wanted to get a coffee with him, I wanted the exchange to continue as if he was the son. I realized that I was making him the son at the same time that he was making me the mother. I thought again of the pond children and inwardly chuckled realizing how they were more my children than this boy should or could ever be.

I was walking in the parking lot alone after the workday. The steering wheel of my car was warm, and my sweaty palms maneuvered it. I realized that I wanted to be maneuvered. I went to the swimming hole again, but now it was a cement, chlorinated pool, a large pool, and the diving board was a high dive. The older children with and without trepidation would run down it and jump or dive. And it was a sumptuous pool into which they jumped or dove, evenly placed within a dominant club. The lights above surrounded it and made the night swim seem exotic. Many were in it now and it was night. Two had their toes touching, entangling on purpose. They did not need to reach for one another since this initial contact was scintillating enough.

I drove home. I wondered about these waters, swimming hole and pool. Neither were lonely. They had company. They were entered to or departed to in time, so there never was too much penetration. As if any measure could determine what that was exactly.

I enter the home wondering what too much penetration is and how blood is not always the measure. The music was playing from speakers that were getting more powerful as they were shrinking in size year after year. He already was home; he chose a light waltz which was strange since I expected jazz. He said it was a light day and he was in a gentle mood.

I took his hand and told him about the time with the red-haired colleague. He moved the story into the waltz, he was graceful, he listened as he moved, and the music was not all mine or his but that bond beyond that encased us each and bore us together.

After the dance, I untied the orange wire holding the plastic bag from getting aired, holding the vegetables I had cut that morning. Did they want steam or oil? A swimming hole has fish swimming along with the people, yet a swimming pool does not. I thought of fish. There was a small amount of swordfish that would go well with these vegetables. I could give him the majority of it, for I only desired a taste.

The knock on the door was not familiar. John answered to the big burly man. The man had on cotton and leather. He knew us but did not remember that. He was here to tell us how we had been cheated. He didn't even have a briefcase or a tie, but he knew all about it. He didn't stay long, he wouldn't have tea, he saw we were midway the swordfish and the vegetables that had been orange-wire tied. We looked over our accounts but waited until the dinner was finished.

The cheating was deliberate though not personal. It wasn't even a shock since we were suspicious when we made the deal. Disconcerting, and there was no way to get around it.

Later that evening in bed, John sleeping evenly with gentle snore beside me, I was thinking of being cheated and the remorse left me, it just slipped right off, like jelly that had been in the sun too long. As it slipped, what was left was the notion that there was nothing that we could have done differently with what we knew then. Then I turned over, my breathing was coming easier yet it wasn't yet sleep. Again, the swimming hole and the pool, the waters, came to me, but now the waters were out of them and were merging, fresh water and chlorinated water were pouring over me or else it was that I was below them as they poured waterfall. Is this a cleansing?

Cleansing from being cheated and then there were the woods by the waterfall and the forts we used to make in the woods; I didn't make them, but I climbed them. And the trees I climbed! I rode my bike to the forts and then I rode it back to home. My bike I called Prince; it was my friend and we moved with speed and balance. And now we are with the children who had been in the swimming hole and in the pool. These children are surrounding my bike and me.

I am wondering who they are, I am about to ask them their names and what they do besides swimming, and then I am sleeping. It all goes out in the wash, some say; water under the bridge, others say. But it is always here and that's the beauty of it. Let them sing those voices for is that not how I found the swimming hole, the swimming pool?

And the next morning, John had left for work after our breakfast, and those voices accompanied me in my walk. The two young men came over in their own time. They were carrying bicycle helmets and a flat bicycle tire. They asked to use our air pump. I was away from home, facing the large field of magenta and yellow and they asked to use our pump. I never found out how they knew we had one.

So, I walked back home with them and still I am not sure why. They were friendly enough, each in his own way. They had different intentions not only this moment with me but in life in general. I could tell that in a few ways: their gait, their posture, the ways their eyes moved and blinked as each spoke. One had the cast of a dark shirt over him, a shirt that had not been washed for a very long time.

When we approached my home, they went straight to the garage and waited for me to get the pump. I asked them where they had left their bikes and if they wanted a lift. They dropped their helmets and said no, they preferred to stay with me that day. What are you possibly meaning? I asked. I don't know you at all - is this some kind of joke or are you about to get violent? I had always surmised that I would keep talking if I ever was in a compromised situation and here I was doing just that.

The one with the cast over him like an unwashed shirt said: We've got no one but one another and we lost our bikes a while ago, exchanged for food and a little money, and this is all we are and all we have.

So, needing air was a ruse? I asked. I don't know what ruse is, ma'am, but it made no sense to keep walking with a flat tire. I picked up on that: And the one or ones who you sold your bikes to - they didn't take that tire? Logic seemed to have nothing to do with the moment, but I persisted. He continued: They told me that the tire was no use to them flat and probably was going to get flat again, so we kept it.

We have no money now, he said.

But you have skill? Still, I was persistent and wondered from where my own questions were coming.

Of sorts, the one without the cast over him replied.

We can plant and harvest, we can work on a grape vine field.

The one cast over reached in his pocket and brought out some change - this is it, all we have and you can have it. You can have all we are.

It didn't take long for me to wonder whether these two were of the children in the watering hole or swimming pool. Are they the older version of who I saw there?

Has there been a water hole, a swimming hole? I asked them, slowly, almost with trepidation.

A long time ago - we'd climb the tree with the rope on it and we'd swing over the pond and jump in for hours. We were happy then.

I have to go to work, I said to them - what will you do?

If you give us something to eat, we'll stay here. He said it as if he was offering me something I needed.

John was in meetings, I'd certainly message him later, but I had to take this on myself at this moment, now.

So, I gave them bread and cheese and some water and drove to work wondering if that was enough. It was not a simple bland naïveté. I had left them outside the house with the doors and windows locked down. I remembered the Bible verses from a very long time ago about the outcasts at our door being Christ, to see Christ in them. But I was not naïve, as I said, I knew I had taken a huge risk and that I had lent myself to something that could be very dangerous.

As I drove, I wondered what their names would be, what would be the names of vagabonds? Already I'm denigrating them, I thought, and they'll probably be gone when I return since they probably detected that attitude.

I messaged my husband that there were two youngish men, vagabonds probably, wanting work. They had wanted to use our air pump for a wheel, though then I found out that their bikes were gone, and they had nothing. John was fine with it all, he said it was something clearly meant to be between me and them and he'd support whatever worked out. Yes, I thought on the ride home, the salient words were 'meant to be' and 'worked out.'

When I drove into our driveway later, I noticed how I was rapidly oscillating between fear and hope. Something in me had already attached to them. I shut the garage door; the sound was so loud that it made an echo. And they were no-where. Oh, I thought, so that was that, just a brief encounter. Yet when I was opening the side door to the home, they were coming from behind suddenly.

I got to look them over for the first time. They were not dis-similar. They had on jeans and shirts that had seen better days as the saying goes. But still there was an air about the one that seemed to have that darker cast over him. I couldn't place it. Some rupture in some place that should have been private and was not, maybe that. I asked them their names - Henry and Michael - not vagabond names. Had the food been enough? I asked as soon as I regretted doing so.

Yes ma'am, the one I knew now as Michael said.

We're mighty tired now though, can we sleep in your garage? He must have noticed that there was a loft over it. It was where we had stored boxes, using it as an attic.

I'll check with John, my husband, but why don't I get you some more food and you can tell me what you think you'd like to do.

With ourselves ma'am? Michael continued to be spokesman. I thought of Aaron and Moses and erased the thought im-mediately; I can't trust them that much.

Well, in the next few days for a start, I said, what do you think you'd like to do?

If you let us stay here, then maybe we can find work.

From where do you come?

From the south, where magnolias are and where we were happy enough until all work was gone when the field where we were working dried up and our folks died, and our relatives wanted nothing to do with us. It smelled sweet down there, ma'am. Honeysuckle and them ripe peaches making it all like a dream. Yep, seems like we, he and I together, had a dream and then we woke up and we were here, in the north, with no more bikes and talking to you ma'am.

I see, I said deliberately and slowly while I imagined my next move.

OK for you to go up and rest in the garage loft for now until John comes home, yet of course, just don't go through anything in there; I'll get blankets and pillows, and something to eat. They were sitting on the lawn while their hands fingered nervously the dirt and grass, as I returned with some cold cuts, more bread and cheese, some orange juice and fruits in a basket, blankets and pillows over my arm. They took them not as greedily as I expected but with what seemed like sincere gratitude.

When John arrived, I knew I had to explain more and didn't like to be in that position - that one of not knowing my own mind and intent and explaining that anyway - to him or anyone.

I went over the morning in detail, the exchanges with them and what had occurred since I had arrived home. He listened without interrupting me and without any movement that would suggest an emotional reaction to what I was saying. When he spoke, he said: I know you're enabling them, their staying here, and being dependent on you and therefore us. So, what is it Megan? - a loneliness of sorts?

Not sure, it's just that they seemed to come out of some waking dreams I was having so I spoke with them. They seemed to be the real-world counterpart of some imaginal reality, so I spoke with them. I'm sorry I communicated with them without consulting you first. It's your home too and we're in it together but there was no time really, it was a split-second sort of moment of decision and action.

I see that, he took my hand, we were sitting now at the kitchen table, and he took my hand on it. But the fact is that we have two vagabonds who are living now over our garage, and, who, therefore, are more or less our responsibility.

I know, and they can rummage through and steal our stored things up there, I know. I would have regrets haunting me forever if that occurred, I know. But can I just tell them to move on tomorrow? The strange thing is, John, that I don't want to -

Our children are grown and out of our lives.

So, you're saying it's a fill in - I'm welcoming the weakest birds from an unfamiliar block to fill a nest too long empty?

Perhaps.

But what if the empty nest called them? What if it's not a defensive filling of what should be hole, but that I was with the hole and they came through that - they are the speaking of the hole?

I think I see. His hand was on his chin now. I thought that this is why I love him so, that 'I think I see' and the hand on the chin.

So, he continued, this is the next phase of the empty nest or hole as you say - this is its logical, or I should say illogical, continuation?

Yes, of sorts.

OK, I'll risk it. I had been wondering what the empty nest was saying to us.

Thank you, I just want to see where it goes and if we get hoodwinked and robbed, well, there's nothing of real value up there, right?

Mostly sentimental but what is mostly there isn't worth anything so wouldn't be of interest to them.

Unless - they wouldn't burn the whole place down? Now I sounded paranoid even to myself, but I was feeling cautious.

Did they seem that sort to you - ?

Not destructive for destruction's sake; they don't seem that desperate or seriously wounded but one never knows these days. The world is volatile and the rages out of raw, unprocessed wounds are often unforeseen.

Agreed, but your instinct took them in - we can trust that, I really think so.

Think or know? I ask it slowly.

Think as in I think it not wonder if.

OK.

****

I awake the next morning with a start. First there was the ending of the dream, a vast futuristic department store, disconcerting in its precise manipulation of the customer, and then the shock of memory of the day before, no mere residue yet the full memory of my encounter and interaction with the two men who now were most likely not only on our property but in our lives.

This shock of memory propelled me into the bathroom where on the toilet I thought it through. The memory moved into the future where it baffled me, so I gave it up and just sat. Pee tinkling and what is this rather different sensation of staying on the pot, not being elsewhere. Perhaps there is something to all this being-in-the-present discourse I think as I wiped myself hopefully clean from the residue of discharging the waste of the day before.

John was already up and had eaten his breakfast; he was in casual clothes for the weekend morning. His mood seemed ordinary and in no way did it suggest perturbation. He was sitting reading the current news and magazines. Piles on the kitchen table became smaller as he read, going through what had stacked up that week. He gave me a smile and hug and in them I could sense he had not forgotten that he had visitors, intruders, or possible guests.

So, are we hosts? I ask him carefully choosing the words and making it plural.

I was going to say, he replied, that you are the host, and this is the result of your moving through and out of your empty nest, but I find I cannot really eliminate myself from it - for that nest empty, as it is or was, had been filled once by starlings of our own, of many forms. And I had told you I would support whatever worked out.

So, what to do now? I asked, surer of the words now.

I suppose I should meet them, he said.

So, I ate since I didn't want to risk such an encounter, which could be difficult or taxing, on an empty stomach. I drank the coffee which I was particular in choosing and brewing.

I'm ready, John said, coming in after walking around the property with his own coffee in hand. I didn't see a sign of them, he said, they must still be in the garage or else they're gone.

I got up and together we walked just there, to the garage, now more a place of curiosity yet we approached with some trepidation. I mentally put myself back on the pot, the toilet of this morning where I was quietly with myself, I found my breath - I saw how I wanted to run from body, from this very breath. I wanted to worry and ruminate to meet the rapidity of heart and the collective angst of so much disturbance through so many lives that I had witnessed and inherited. But the angst let go finally - was it something about these two men and meeting them that allowed this letting go as much as it had caused the very angst? No time to wonder and the repetition of my breathing moved me upstairs alongside my husband.

I thought I heard drumming when I reached the top stairs. Was it from my heart or from the outside? I took John's arm for a moment to steady myself. Then he opened the door to the loft.

They were, well the best description would be lounging on the blankets and pillows surrounded by boxes filled with our lives before and during our marriage. Remnants and whole albums and accounts of our days from childhoods onwards. Here is what surrounded Henry and Michael.

They were awake, Henry more than Michael. Both were just looking mostly up mostly at the ceiling which was A shaped and needed attention as did much of the garage.

It was Michael, not surprisingly, who spoke once our presence aroused him more: We could sheet rock this loft for you, then it wouldn't let in rain, snow, wind and be safe for your boxes. I wager that you want to keep them safe and dry? Memories are like that, he added, we want to keep them yet not right in the face of us but not wet and soggy and gone completely.

This latter sentence took both John and I by surprise. It was rather deep and thoughtfully worded. This is my husband John, I said to them both. John, here is Henry, here is Michael, pointing to them respectively. They each half sat up to shake his hand. I registered that neither stood.

But then they did stand up and I took them in more fully as John was telling them what I had relayed to him about the meeting the three of us had had the day before.

Henry was broad shouldered and rather stooped, he had a rag-like cloth over one shoulder, a red plaid shirt with a tear in the bottom that hung over brown, very loose fitting carpenter pants that had what looked like grease stains up and down them, in various abstract designs. His feet were bare now but crumbled gray socks lay near shoe-boots that were cracking in places.

When I looked at Michael, I saw immediately that he had attempted to look more coherent: his jeans were not ripped or marked yet very worn, and he was quickly tucking his shirt inside them as he stood to speak. The shirt was a heavy cotton and when clean would probably be a light blue. Both of them had hair below their ears and, other than a similar shape of their mouths, it would be difficult to tell that they were brothers, if they were.

Are you two brothers? I asked at this first break in the conversation which was more prolonged than I would have expected. Cousins, but we've known one another for a very long time and it's like brothers. So, we're like brothers, ma'am. Here was Michael speaking. He had been the one who had spoken to John; yet still not a word yet from Henry.

Where you from boys? John asked with a tone that for him was quite engaging and open.

I noticed that as Michael began to speak, Henry was twisting what looked like a piece of paper in his hands.

Minnesota. But we're a long way from there and we're looking for a new area, yes ma'am, a new area to settle down and be fruitful members of society.

Minnesota didn't connect with what they had talked about coming from the South, but I remained quiet.

You boys in trouble with the law or anything? It was a reasonable question, and I knew John would ask it eventually, yet I also knew it was a question that could not possibly be answered in the positive.

We're finished with that, Michael said slowly, marking each word while his cousin simultaneously nodded.

But then a strange thing happened, or, given the strangeness of the entire context, perhaps it was just more unexpected within the strangeness. Henry made a dash to leave. Whether he was leaving the questioner or himself in the question - all that was uncertain, yet John was the first to react.

Whoa son!
It came as a surprise to us all yet particularly to me that Henry actually stopped and turned around.

John continued: We're here to help. We're not the sort to send men who are in need out to the claws of the world.

He usually wasn't so poetic yet that phrase 'claws of the world' was apt and rang a few times in my innermost heart.

I joined in - yes, claws of the world is right, you both clearly are in need of some sustenance, we can offer you that until you get your feet on the ground, as they say.

We'd be obliged ma'am and sir, Michael said seemingly for them both though his look to his cousin was inquisitive.

Henry ripped the twisted piece of paper and looked directly at Michael. The stare was not only direct and intense, it wanted something. There was such a want in that stare that I could not remain standing. I sat on the boxes nearby.

John spoke then: Maybe we should take this to the kitchen. I imagine you both could do with a cup of coffee.

My husband had invited them into our house. What could he see, what was he seeing that I was not? Before he had been so cautious.

This acceptance that we have been cut and lost what was part of our earlier being. It was like Henry was dealing with that and Michael was not or perhaps Henry was struggling for the two of them. Michael and John continued to speak on the way into the house and I hung back with Henry. Partly I wanted to see if he'd run away though I was sure he wouldn't part permanently with his cousin; I wanted to see if he'd run to hide or just leave the situation for a time, leave the interaction which seemingly demanded so much of him.

So, Henry and I walked into the kitchen behind the other two, silently. He still had that cloth over his shoulder. John was getting down the mugs. I asked them if they'd like to use the lavatory. Beforehand, I thought of the pills in the cabinet but asked anyway. Michael went straightaway. I could tell Henry could not withstand being alone with us, so I offered him the second bathroom and showed him the way.

When I returned to John, I lifted the eyebrow that he knew meant the question of what the hell are we doing. He said: It will be OK. Let's just take it slowly and keep calm. There were five other relevant questions I wanted to discuss with him, but Michael already was coming back with Henry at his heels.

We sat around the table as if we had invited friends over for breakfast. I made toast, bacon, and eggs. Michael brought up the option of sheet rocking again. John replied that that might be a possibility and asked them if they had family.

Everyone we cared about is gone.

Henry, still silent, was eating slowly yet clearly enjoying the food. He seemed to be shuffling his feet and I thought at first it was done out of a certain frustration but then realized it more was the delight in the meal, a delight he could not as yet word.

Then the four of us sat there for what seemed like twenty minutes. It may have been two minutes or even one minute in actuality. There was some strain within the fabric of this silence, at least for me, and from what I could perceive. I felt it as a pull at my stomach. But I knew not to break it defensively from an inability to withstand it. Yet I did want to swing my foot, I noticed how some parts of my body want to discharge, deliver this tension out of my body and out of the room.

Instead, I quieted. What helped was to go elsewhere in my mind while there. It was a beach with sand so fine and white it looked pink in the full beating sun. There were umbrellas and mothers and toddlers and children all around. Convivial play in ocean waters in the hot sun. Sun fire and water washing was where I was going but then I stopped and looked around me: John there, Michael, Henry - all in very different stances and postures regarding this silence. For Michael, it seemed absolutely to be oppressive; I thought I noticed a tic below his right eye.

For John, it was uncomfortable, but he was using the silence to appraise the situation. Our eyes met. The contact of these four eyes told me immediately that he was figuring things out and was not completely sure yet. I told him in this contact that I understood completely.

Yet for Henry, this silence had a different effect altogether. He was upright in his chair, looking down at the table and unequivocally at ease. In fact, it was the most at ease that I had seen him since he first had appeared the day before. His eyes were no longer shifting, there was no twisting of paper, not a muscle in his body seemed to move either in defense or a necessity of any kind.

Finally, John spoke. He looked in their general direction and asked them what their plans were after all. What I mean, he said, is even if you do sheet rock our garage - and that would be a good idea for us to have done if not now then at some point - even if you do it, what then? What after that - where do you want to go?

I registered that he did not say: Where are you going - but instead he went for the intent. I waited expecting Michael to speak. But perhaps the silence that unnerved us three in various ways refreshed the fourth since it was Henry who spoke. We know our basic way, sir.

No need to call me sir, John said almost too instantly adding - John is fine. But the moment was gone or lost. Henry looked down and said nothing. So, Michael took over: He means, John, that we'll be fine, you don't have to concern yourselves about us after we're through here.

Through here - had an ominous ring, but it may have been that the silence had worked on me to a considerable extent. I deliberated whether to speak, whether to get up, whether to be in that vicinity at all. Michael, as it seemed he was wont to do, solved my questioning by sweeping his chair away from his body, standing and beginning to collect the dishes. He even asked if he could get us more coffee.

Whether it was again the effect of silence or not, I thought it particularly strange to be asked such in my own kitchen and I noticed that I was tightening, closing down.

No, that's fine, I said in my cheery, higher voice used when I needed to run for cover. I'll finish up here. Why don't you two take your coffee outside and John and I will join you soon. The door closed behind them, and I sat back down looking at my husband differently than I had done in the eye contact through the intense silence. This look was furtive and signaled more fear.

What are we getting ourselves into? I noticed an edge of panic in my voice that I hadn't had for a while. Now John was taking the position I originally had: he was more grounded and almost optimistic in the decision about them. They're not going to hurt us, he said, I really sense that, but it's true that that silence was eerie.

Yes, certainly eerie. It's that Henry, I added, but did you notice how the silence seemed to calm him and allow him to communicate?

I saw it - I felt it more - but that is what opened me more to a favorable view of them, he said. How so? I asked. Well, it's the quiet behind their presentation - the Henry behind the Michael so to speak that's the issue, could be the problem, don't you think?

Yes - but that silence was, I agree, eerie, so the silence is what discomforted me.

But it didn't unsettle Henry. He was fine in it, even more 'human' if you will.

I don't see it; I don't see what assured you in that. Anyway - I asked John then the question one could call ultimate - Do we hire them or not and where will they stay?

No problem for them to sleep up there where they'll be working. Maybe I can get them other jobs around here too.

They appeal to you or is it your compassion for the underdog, which usually is strong, coming to the fore?

I don't know, he said, but I know I won't let them hurt you or us.

I don't think that's in my hesitancy now - it's not physical harm that is on my heart but psychological intrusion. We are letting other wounded beings into our atmosphere where the question of taking on the wound is ever present and, maybe more for me than you, pressing.

Gender differences after all? He said this lightly as lightly as he put his arms around me gracefully and without encumbrance.

So, we went out to them and hired them. There were trips to get the sheet rock and materials; there were trips to the grocery for more food, food for four. The nest was being revived like those that lay dormant on a window sill and are almost devastated by the winter storms but then enough twigs intertwined with nestling fur remain through it all, so once again, maybe not the next year but in two years, they get rebuilt and the chirping song returns as if never halted, through the generations, the song, Ruth's, hidden missal, nightingale.

I say it 'was,' the nest was being revived; I didn't say we rebuilt it.

****

When Iris came over for coffee the following week, she was curious about the noises coming from the garage, the general sense of new work in what had been a very settled and settling home. Often these coffee updates were on more surface occurrences, but she sensed immediately that there was more to the noise than carpenters hired for a job.

Maybe my hand trembled minutely as I poured the coffee. Maybe I wasn't as oriented to her as usual or interested in the details of her events during the last couple of weeks. Perhaps I wasn't remembering, as I usually do, the details she had relayed during our last visit. In any case, she asked about who they were in there, in our garage, and their significance.

These two were there, I told her, just there and I engaged with them and then John returned and was suspicious and then we exchanged perspectives, he and I: I became worried and didn't even want to hire him and now he's out trying to get them other jobs. But they're here, sleeping where they work, drifters it seems. Can you believe it?

She tapped her cup with the forefinger of her right hand a few times before she spoke. I couldn't do it, she said, but I'm swamped with grandkids and rides here and there and sports games and school plays that make me want to come home to quiet. She chuckled looking at me to make sure that I could relax into this conversation with her.

She was a hefty lady, my friend, and not encumbered by and without excuse for her weight, for the space she took, for her ability to be at peace in her body. I suppose I relied on her for this body peace. But now she was telling me she couldn't do it for other reasons too: she would be too worried about invasion and harm. It's just the way these days, they get envious and mad and strike out and seize what they can, she added.

Now I got even more worried that we had made a huge mistake and that my husband was being deceived and, while he was unaware of that, a blanket of deception was over the entire home, and we were living beneath it unaware that oxygen was depleting.

I expressed these fears to her.

Well, it's like you both went into a jungle for an adventure since the house got so quiet and then you brought the jungle back in.

But I wasn't looking for it, I was aware of the emptiness and processing it for a while and then they were there.

Like sent?

Yes actually. Aren't we related to everyone in our path, isn't that what we have to work on next in the extension of ourselves to be who we are supposed to be? And I wasn't defensively filling it, you know that, and you witnessed me being OK in the aloneness, John and I in the aloneness.

That's true, that's true. I'm wrong about the jungle. You were in the emptiness authentically. OK, if it is a gift or a presentation on or expression of what you have to take in next, so to speak, who sent it and why?

That's the question. Or should I even be asking such? Maybe it's just a question of how it is we are with them, how we can communicate with them and find who they are for us and with us and apart from us.

I see, she said, just what still worries me is that there are only two possible versions of this story: either they do a good job and you get them work with compassionate neighbors or there's a breach and you get hurt or die.

Already they have asked for more work here – they say that they can reinforce the structure of the garage.

Hmm - what about the fact of the two versions - does that say anything to you?

Yes, even for someone who works at not getting caught by such contraries, undoing the dichotomies to see their inter-change and intention - yes, it does seem like two possible versions: we're exceptionally generous and empathic to for-eign souls or we're fools and get damaged. But what if we are having to look at our own damage, those places which are almost beyond words and ailing and pleading? What if that is what is in the emptiness?

I see. I have to go, but we'll continue. I'll call daily for a while. I thanked her as I shut the door behind her.

The following morning when I first opened my eyes, I re-called the conversation with Iris, and I thought it all had been a dream - two strange men living over our garage. So, the first words to my husband were: Are you sure?

So far so good was the reply before he got up to his morning ablutions. Then we spoke more. The sheet rocking was nearly done, without incident. They were tidy enough with their work and it was clear that the job was well done and would be a necessary protective cover for our stored belongings as well as the cars below.

So, you were right about the sheet rocking, I said. But another job? They've not said much of anything to us this entire time. I was making coffee. Even when I bring meals out to them, it's just thank you, ma'am.

You sound annoyed, he said nonchalantly.

It's a weight. They're quiet, they're neat, but I feel as though a granite boulder is over our home, the heaviness of their presence - well, I find it rather taxing really.

He huddled some in his chair, thinking, the thinker.

I sense it too, he finally said. And I know we're not supposed to chisel through or smash through that granite but it's what has been given to us, without solicitation, as you said earlier, that's for sure.

So, I suppose, I conceded, we should ask what the granite wants from us, for us.

Grounding us? Now he was asking the questions.

Yesterday Iris and I spoke of empty nest. I discussed with her the way we may have to look into our own damage, that which is beyond words yet wanting to be spoken, felt and known.

So, in our empty nest we are shown that our damage is like a granite boulder over us, he said. But at some point or another it's time to just leave the nest, our work as parents is done there, why stay? Certainly, it is not to fill it with granite.

Should we go to the mountain then? Is it the grandfather calling Heidi?

Or is it Heidi yearning for grandfather? Now he was going inward deeply with me.

Or is it just to be like granite, sturdier, solid.

Yet granite can be the drugged elderly in nursing homes, heavy and stupefied.

That granite is hopefully not ours. Nursing home without drugs, maybe, but still opening to a stillness more the rock of ages. Just that steady mass of so many brown hues.

Strangely enough, to the surprise of us both, it was Henry at the door. We were almost too shocked to speak or move.

He certainly seemed like granite. Not a muscle on his moved. Was he even knocking?

Henry? I found the voice to ask.

It's me. He replied.

Can we do something for you? Again, in my voice.

Do you want to come in Henry? John's voice.

No, I just wanted you to know Michael got himself hurt and he ran off into the woods. I don't know where to go.

What? I said it, but John made the first move. He dashed out to the edge of the trees bordering our property. There was the walk that deer and fawn took during the liminal times of the day and that more menacing creatures took at night or, aberrantly, during the daylight. I heard the name called repetitively: Michael, Michael, Michael. We can help you, come back, we're here!

We're here. Henry actually was mumbling it. Here, here, hear. And he pointed to his right ear. I thought I saw blood in it. Bleeding in the ear - what could that be? Is this loss of his other self, his more verbal adapted Michael self, triggering some blood memory?

Come back, I heard myself saying to Henry: It's OK, we'll find him, you're not alone, that's what John meant by we're here.

Henry looked at me in a flash that was quicker than that of my insight about his blood and ear - actually a brilliant flash it was. The sort that allowed me to see all the intelligence that was numbed out in him. Then he was back to looking to the ground and shuffling his feet and refusing to come inside the house.

It was cozy in there with the smells and general warmth of the after-breakfast atmosphere. It was like those minutes after a fine conjugal sleep where one was awake finally to the prescience of the dawn. Yet he would not enter. No warm echoes of union when his brother in soul was nowhere to be known.

But our quick exchange was calming for him: I could see it, he visibly let down some and his body armor changed to a metal more pliable. It was not that the armor went but that its form remained with a different tone and substance.

John returned with some twigs in his right hand. He said that his call returned empty. He threw the twigs down, empty handed.

He continued: We can't scout those woods just the two of us but we can get help or we can sit and wait. I really think he'll be back in his own time. He is truly caring of Henry - he won't abandon him.

Or us? It was a question in our minds simultaneously that neither voiced.

Let's do both, he said. I'll call Gary and Tom and we'll go out in three directions. Why don't you stay here with Henry.

I immediately thought: That will be interesting. John saw it in my face. Then he was off. Henry was still at the door. He had obeyed the Here, Here, Hear. I thought I saw that his ear was just trickling a few drops of blood now. I stood there with him and waited for it to end. I knew, of course, that it was in my mind, yet it certainly seemed as though he too was aware of it - he bent his head ever so lightly in the direction of the said falling trickle.

Then he did something that I would say was unexpected, but everything was unexpected at this point. He unwrapped and took off his belt. He handed it to me. He always had seemed like an orphan to me, but this action cemented it.

I put the belt on the kitchen chair and returned to the door, to him. I thought that the gesture meant that he was relinquishing what I would see as his aggression. I may have been totally off with this guess, but it seemed to suit and even relax me. And he still was calm since I had not reacted negatively to the gesture.

So, there we stood. A threshold to our home between me and the guest who, in the way he took and warranted my attention that was moving more to esteem, was becoming more host. I don't know whether he had this post since I gave it to him or not, but now he definitely had the power in our dyad.

Then I thought I saw a hunter green tin cup in his left hand, the sort one would take camping. I asked him if he'd like a drink of water while we waited for Michael to return. His cheek tinged at the name but then he nodded. I went into the kitchen to get some in a mug and, when I returned, he was gone.

Oh God, two lost, and I checked my emotional response. I would have predicted a sort of relief, but it was not that at all. I missed him in the way I would if someone had given me a small but relevant gift and then it disappeared.

Actually, I miss them both, I realized, as I cantered to the garage. And there he was, sitting on slabs of wood and waiting for his drink. I went back to the house to get it, brought it to him and handed it to him. He nodded, or more accurately, his eyebrows nodded. I point to the spot next to him on his right. He nodded this time with a more full-headed nod. Then I sat beside him.

I looked around. It was a garage that John had overstuffed with tools, machines, remnants and promises yet kept all in a neat array. I rubbed my eyebrows, put my head in my hand as Henry finished the water. I looked up at the rafters, beams supporting the loft above as well as various stored items once appraised by my husband as save-worthy.

I wished there was a chimney there with a hearth. I really wanted there to be a hearth as I sat beside Henry. There was just so much silence that verged on being cold in myself though I knew he was not cold, and, strangely enough, was even warm in it. But one thing his silence did seem to want was a home. I don't have it in me to provide such, I thought. But that's just your thought. Someone had answered me. I looked at Henry who was just as immobile and still as ever. Who had spoken to me? I looked around in my head - it came, I realize, from the place where the vision of the blood-from-the-ear had come. It was a women's voice.

Say again? I asked her. But that's just your thought. So, I asked: Are you saying that I have such a hearth for Henry? The hearth of a home...

For you all, she replied.

Where - where can there be a home for such a soul emerging from such emptiness?

She replied: Whether empty nest or just human loneliness, the hearth can be accessed and is burning through souls loved surrounding you. And the angel. And the saints.

And the angel and the saints? I asked. She elaborated: Souls surrounding you including the saints and the angel.

Guardian angel?

You call it such. There are other groups also. But they pull like a magnet the souls of loved ones to and around you, supporting, fueling, yes, as are the saints, keeping the hearth. All ordained.

Damn. I thought it through and realized that what this voice said was for the good and the common good; I was discerning that it was not out of destruction. I then thought of the answer to the biblical question: who is my neighbor?

Henry was shuffling his feet now though not actually moving anywhere.

Can you hear her? I asked Henry.

He nodded though I really was not sure he understood the question. So, I asked further: What do you make of it?

I am cold now, he said.

Perhaps the first words he spoke to me alone since we met.

Come with me, I said clearly and with a mixture of gentleness and firmness that surprised even me as did the way he got right up and followed me back to the door of the kitchen.

I brought a chair from the table over to the threshold for him to sit upon and, after he went through the doorway to it, I shut the door right behind him. I motioned to it and, surprising me again, he sat. Then I pointed to the stove upon which was a kettle. He nodded and I made the tea. I thought to put it in a teacup instead of a mug.

He held it cupped by both palms, warming himself and then he took a small sip, warming his mouth and throat. He grunted. I had settled myself considerably. The hearth was here.

His ankles were crossed beneath his chair. Now he seemed to be digesting the tea, his head bent, focused on its course warming him centrally and emanating out in a way that I hoped would allow some words to find their way to me.

So, I sat quietly and then I gave him another cup. I was wondering if Michael and the men were well on their way through the woods.

Time seemed to stretch itself to our need. And our need was for us to become more familiar in our accompanying one another. I noticed his eyebrows were hairy and wondered if that had been the case since he was a young adult. I noticed his socks actually matched and then felt guilt at the supposition that they would not.

Nots came and went in fact in this time of Henry drinking the hot tea: he is not as strange as I had thought; it is not going to be easy to communicate with him with words particularly without Michael here; this room is not as altered with his presence in it as I had thought it would be; I am not wary of him any longer; I do not want him to leave.

In fact, his presence had become almost mesmerizing. There was a sense of decay in it which I was trying to locate. It was just a sense of something deep in his being that had died and onto which he held.

Let it go Henry, I found myself whispering.

He stopped sipping and I worried for a moment that he would think I had meant the cup.

Not risking breakage either of the cup or more importantly of my connection with him, I said: Not the cup.

I know. Two more words. His voice was not as cracked and dry as I had supposed it could be, would be.

I'd like a piece of that pie.

He must have seen it on the counter, half eaten, though at no time had I noticed him looking in that direction.

As I heated up the pie and prepared a dish, I heard him speak more words: I worry for the country.

I'm not sure I follow you, I told him as I handed him the dish.

He began to eat the pie slowly, savoring.

You must be hungry. I should have offered you more - would you like more to eat?

Head shake no. Very concise.

The country, I continued, is darkening but there may be a pause - I pray for it. I understand your and Michael's wandering in the face of such times.

At the name of his cousin, he jolted. China plate with pie stayed intact though was rattling.

It had all gotten too noisy. I silenced. The aroma of the pie, the pie all but forgotten in the activities and worries of the last two days, now was surrounding me thoroughly. I got up and got a piece of it for myself. I was letting the hearth refuel, I realized.

There was a noise from the porch, at first, I was thinking John was returning yet also thought how that would be too soon - I wanted more time with Henry, or the soul of Henry which was more what I was encountering.

Then his strange words: Put on an apron and, when you cook, food won't spoil your outfit.

Well, I wasn't planning on cooking for a while unless you are hungry?

He shook his head no and looked down, it seemed that he was embarrassed.

Is that what happened to you? Something spilled on you?

I thought of the connection with the word spoil and the sense of decay.

No, shaking his head again.

I thought of popcorn for some reason and almost chuckled. Is this like being in a movie I had thought I was watching? The night was quickly approaching though it seemed like it was not even noon.

Time passed as my experience of it revved up.

I wanted an apple, I wanted something to crunch.

I got up and got one and indeed the crunching seemed to be at a regular time and pace and the wet sourness felt good going down, being within me.

Then Henry stood and put the plate on the counter next to his empty teacup near the sink. He looked like he could lean against the counter but then he stood upright and put both hands in his pockets. The he turned and began to go to the door.

Henry, don't leave yet please. John will call or return soon, and we'll have news.

His hand was on the door, and he opened it. He turned back and smiled. And then he was gone.

To the garage again - right? - I ran after him - you're just going to the garage, right? I yelled out to him.

But he went by it.

I kept running after him.

Fortunately, he was not a swift mover, and I increased my pace to catch up with him. I knew not to speak. I thought for an instant that he might spring forward into a canter and perhaps he might have considered such for a split second. But then he stopped. We were standing side by side in the same looking forward direction.

I felt myself about to weep without a clue why or from what source such tears were coming. Were they his as well? Still standing alongside this immensely quiet and I surmised quietly perturbed man, I had an image going across my head from right to left. I saw the two of us sitting on the ground face to face both cross-legged. At first, we are not looking at one another at all but gradually, after a long time, in the image it is dusk, and we do. There is not an ounce of romance in it. And I hear the words in my head: don't get me wrong, don't get me wrong.

Then I imagine a ballerina with a torn tutu; she looks surprised and completely dismayed. And at the point I am looking at Henry who still is looking straight ahead as if my images had no effect on him. But actually, I think they do.

For he looks down on the ground and then says in a voice deeper than before: Michael.

I want to soothe or pity him as I check that impulse knowing it false and constrain myself from doing either. Let's go back to the kitchen, I say to him, that's the best place to wait.

Best? He is asking me and now he looks at me; what I had thought was his dishevelment falls away and I see a very serious man looking at me. He is not looking me over or looking into me, but he is looking in my direction and seems to see my eyes looking back at him.

John may be there now, I think, and I also think of the bizarre custom of crossing fingers solidifying a wish. Henry follows me back to the house. Yet as I open its door the kitchen has an emptiness that I don't remember it ever having to that degree. No John, no Michael, but even less than that, there are fewer inhabitants than before, saints and angels all have departed it seems. No wonder Henry did not want to come in before. And now? I turn around and he is close behind me. I just keep walking in, it's useless to ask him to do anything else, and I know it. I hear the screen door close behind me and he takes his hand off its handle. He is who shuts the door, we are inside.

We are in this empty room with four walls, a floor and a ceiling and the emptiness is of such magnitude that it has made invisible as well as irrelevant the four walls, floor, and ceiling.

Suddenly, I feel nauseous. I excuse myself and go into the bathroom. I sit on the toilet, clothes still on and put my head in my hands. Swimming head not bolstered by any hand. For a second, I think he's come to the door, listening, and that second is within a startle that takes me by surprise. Whatever you want God please make it manifest. Stomach and head swim in opposite directions, useless hands. This magnitude of emptiness.

I open the bathroom door and there is no one there and I slowly return to what had been my kitchen. The faucet either had been dripping and I hadn't noticed it, or else Henry might have run it for a drink and didn't close it enough. He is still standing up as still as he had been before.

Then his voice, deep and slow: Are you sick?

It's the room, I say to him, it's changed.

I noticed. Is it because of me? Has me being here made you sick?

I want to politely and immediately disagree, but I honestly do not know the answer to that question.

I think it's been a long day, I say. It's the closest I can get to the truth.

I think of wreaths then, Spring wreaths, just two of them being prepared for front doors. Made by the soft, agile hands of those foreign.

It doesn't do to inquire why now this image, I thought, but I let it stay before me. Two floral wreaths being prepared by foreign women. These women are poor and incredibly artistic and skilled. I keep thinking they should be sad due to their circumstances, historically and at the present, but they are not. They are reconciled and glad to be doing work in fair trade.

I blink my eyes to orient back to Henry. He is related to the images after all and I'm not sure how, but it doesn't matter.

I know that attending to these images is helping me be with him and know how to be with him. I experience a softness in my being that wasn't there before with him. So, I trust these 'visiting' images and words more.

I then imagine Michael coming through the kitchen door and he looks happy. I want to ask him where John is. All this time, Henry is standing still. I ask him if he'd like another cup of tea. He tells me he did have a drink of water when I was in the bathroom.

How such a wounded, reticent man would take the initiative to do so perplexes me. I have to remember how strange this man is and stop this soft regard I'm developing to him. He could be dangerous.

But such a word makes no sense any longer. It does not fit the man, or even the space around him. The time when that word had had an application in my heart has passed.

Two humans in outer space, inside.

Then I manage to have us sit at the kitchen table, mostly through gesture. We are sitting with the corner between us: me at the head of the table and Henry at my right-side diagonal to the head. He is moving his finger across part of the table directly in front of him. He seems to be mumbling.

What? I ask. He shakes his head no. But I heard the word Michael. I think: will Michael be permanently gone? What will happen in this generation if the Michaels who are the protectors and the voice of the Henrys go?

There is a type of scurrying at the door. Sounding like a chipmunk but higher on the door. I imagine a child dressed as a clown and smiling. Is it a good or bad clown? Whose joke have I entered? I remain sitting and, strange to me at least, it is Henry who goes to the door. He has his hand on the knob and then turns around to face me.

Open it, I say, it's OK.

He turns the knob. I see an arm, a man is lying on the ground and reaching up; he had been scratching the door, he is ill, I see blood on his hand. It is Michael. I rush to the door. I kneel down to him, this visitor no longer stranger yet now so clearly not himself.

He has scratches and tears all over him, he has been torn. He is musically inclined however - even in his disarray and pain - he is humming. The rhythm may be soothing him though I find it irregular and almost frightening.

Henry is lifting him. Michael resists at first and then he re-
laxes into the hold which seems caring, genuinely affection-
ate, the most feeling I've seen emanate from the stranger
man now carrying this body in pain into the kitchen and now
the living room and, with a furtive glance in my direction
asking if the couch can be covered to collect any blood. I rush
to get two towels and Michael is placed sensitively on them.

I look at his face for the first time - it is very scratched and
beginning to swell in places. His eyes, once so clear and penetrating, are rimmed in what looks like soot and the whites
of his eyes are more red than white. Red veins in those eyes
beseech me. They ask me: Where were you? How long have
I known you? Then a simple, also unexpected question:
Where is my father?

I am not your mother, I say though unsure from where those
words are coming in me. I am not your mother, but I can
clean you and get you some medical help.

I see that I have reverted to a posture and voice almost un-
recognizable to myself: the sort that comes in a shock when
one is outside a hospital waiting during surgery and there are
only a few minutes to communicate to a relative what has
transpired over years.

That overload is in the posture, this posture, this voice saying
I can get you medical help.

That won't be necessary. He is responding; he is sitting on
the couch.

I want to go into the bathroom. I want to simplify this situation. I want to be less overloaded. I do not know where John
is or why he isn't at this moment by my side or whether he
too is in any sort of trouble.

I remain kneeling at the couch. Henry has gotten wet cloths
at my direction and now I tell him where to get glasses for a
glass of water. Michael drinks the water and the eyes looking
at me over the glass are becoming more his own. Henry's vi-
talization in the face of Michael's unraveling is noteworthy.
I am saying such words as that in my mind: noteworthy. That
would be funny if we all were not in such a strange situation.

Then there seems to be a long table set in the living room and
it is an organic feast. Salads, hors d'oeuvres, vegetables,
fruits. Brimming without delicacies. Hearty, healthy. Michael is feeding. But it is a fleeting wish, not like the other
images that I had been given. I look at Michael sitting up on
the couch covered with towels and ask him: Where is John?

I thought he was here, with you.

He went to look for you.

I came back myself.

I rushed to the kitchen door and looked frantically about, calling my husband over and over until I realized the futility of such. I clung to the aluminum handle of the screen door; it was cold and, strangely, damp, almost soft. I looked around again, mentally walked up and down the driveway, and came back to the cold, damp handle. I was in a state between frozen and numbness and not sure why. Certainly, John knew his way home from wherever he was, and he and his friends would find their way. What is this panic? After a brief look around the kitchen, I went back into the living room. They were gone. The front door was not completely shut.

But I did not move. I stayed frozen and numb and totally without thought of any kind. It may have been five minutes, or it may have been an hour. I may have been sitting or standing. There were no people, no pets, no plants even to associate with and through. The familiar furniture was not speaking, yet it did hold me. This living room, this parlor, held me.

I was not even aware of blinking. And there were no images but an evenly penetrating sound benevolent and as if emanating from the holding living room. The sound within the unique images of each time.

Much later, still sitting yet more cognizant of sitting, I heard that aluminum latch. His footsteps, those sounds which had been my first introduction to him long ago, that specific beat, were coming upon me.

His arm was around me. He told me that Michael was nowhere to be found. He looked around the room. He saw the blood on the towels, and he asked me where Henry was. I couldn't speak but I was at a peace which would remain in our bond and had enveloped two swallows gifting us this sound that filled.

****

It was a long conversation transpiring far into the night. We were deciding what to do as we were secretly staying up waiting for them to return. We both knew that to follow them out into the night would be of no avail and would exhaust us and defeat any effort to think through how to respond in ways beneficial to us all. But we could not just turn off the light and go to bed either. And neither of us got up to shut the front door completely either. By this time, it had a far too symbolic meaning to do so.

There we sat on the couch knees touching and felt their loss and the loss of them and spoke to one another about possible strategies, plans to recover them, but then the loss returned and ended those words and we fell into that quiet peace that the two had left with us.

Maybe that is what this all is - I broke the silence - maybe it was just about them getting a rest, nourishment, and some money, and leaving us to go to their next stop. And, in exchange, we have been given this sense of quiet that they live within.

But, he said, one is hurt, and the other is certainly not fit for this world. He said it in a practical tone which did not completely cover the undercurrent of concern and anxiety.

I thought then that perhaps this degree, this form and texture, of the quiet was their gift to me primarily. Perhaps it was not for John so much, and, when presented, not accepted or seen as crucial to his being. Perhaps we have different "vocations" in being given what can complete us more.

So, I attended to his concerns as I did to my own. He expressed his main question: Why did Michael run off in the first place? Why did he run? How could he just leave, never mind only us, but also Henry?

Perhaps that's it - I spoke as I was thinking it out - when he was the one more wounded, he couldn't be with his cousin since the main way of his being with Henry was to be the one not wounded or not as wounded...? He had to be the helper, the do-er, the speaker, the one connecting his cousin to the world, or he couldn't be with him.

And he knew, John added, that Henry was in good hands.

He took my hands as he said: We should really go to bed and shut the front door.

I'd rather sleep down here tonight, and I think you'd prefer that also. Don't worry - I'll sleep fine here.

So, we each got on a couch and pulled afghans over us. As usual, his snoring was not obtrusive enough to prevent my falling to sleep and even may have been helping that, but then I went to all the possible places the two may be this night and I barely slept.

There was no sound in the morning: no scratching at any door, no hammering in the garage, no creaking of a cautious step on any of our wooden floors.

We decided to both take the day off from work and we sat at the kitchen table after eating, wondering what next.

Eventually, John went out to the garage, and I stayed at the table and went inside myself to where I knew them, particularly Henry, in that silence. I was moving through its ominous layers and going deeper to where there was no annoyance or thrill or fear, but just abiding, being there in a way that reached out to all silence.

I did find him there. He was not afraid. He was cuddled. He cuddled next to his cousin and seemed to give the other the warmth from this deep level of silence, and that warmth was protective of Michael in his woundedness.

I stood up, brought the dishes to the sink and began washing them when the kitchen door opened, and John came in. I could tell by the look on his face that he had found them. Where? I asked.

They never left the house really. They were huddled at the base of the tree overhanging the back of the garage, leaning against it and the wood shingles.

I gasped - where are they now?

They're still there. I saw them when I was leaving the garage, I went over to them. Hello boys, I said, glad to see you. They didn't move. Michael was behind Henry and didn't even look at me which was strange since he usually was talkative to us.

I'll go out - I dried my hands, went to John; we hugged and from that moment of sustenance I took out what plentitude I had in Spirit to those two. John agreed to stay in the kitchen.

I found them and it was as John had described: two huddled beings in a reverse order of power than that in which we had known them. I began to say: Henry, it's so great of you to take care of Michael that way… but then I realized that such most likely would make Michael veer away more, ashamed he couldn't do his job, the one set out for him for so long, caretaker, speaker, the one in charge.

So, I didn't say anything. The time alone in the kitchen had allowed me to stay in Henry's silence so within that I approached them. I bent to the base of the tree and put my arms around them both. There we were three huddled souls of the crevice between tree and garage.

It could have been two minutes or thirty seconds. Then I sat down right there with them. None of us had looked at the other yet. I realized I never really had looked right at their eyes. My glance always had had an angle in it, just barely missing the eyes without any desire to go there.

So, I moved to where I could sit before Henry and then I looked at him, looked into his eyes. I realized they had hazel tints but that wasn't what I saw or looked at: looking at his eyes was also to look into them. A vast terrain was there, rugged, hardly trespassed, open, and not barricaded in any way.

I had never traversed such a space before, certainly it seemed alien. But it was before me and my time with this man had prepared me for the first steps into it.

As I did step into it, Michael began to move. He just shifted a bit, but that was enough to tell me that if I could take his role with his cousin, he could revive more.

So, Michael began to get up. I looked up at him. He looked down at me and smiled, I could sense his gratitude. Then we helped Henry up and went into the kitchen.

John was making fresh coffee. We took our places at the kitchen table, and I began to smile as I noted how automatic that activity was: that we indeed did have, each of us, our own place at this table.

The two were looking down at the table. They each were disheveled and dirty after the night out and the events of the day before. I looked at Michael's hand. It had a diagonal gash along the top going towards the palm between the forefinger and the thumb. That should be looked at, I said.

No hospitals or doctors. He spoke for himself now. It didn't cut a nerve, I'm OK now.

Yet, John said, it needs to be cleaned up. Look, he continued, why don't you each take a bathroom and shower and then we'll look at that cut and bandage it.

Or, I spoke tentatively, would you rather eat first, you must be starving.

To our surprise, it was Henry who took the lead. He stood up and walked towards the bathroom and Michael followed him, going upstairs, to the second one. They each took long showers in the warm waters of our well.

While they were showering, I looked at John. Almost simultaneously we shrugged. I then stood and began making a large breakfast. John thought of the issue of their dirty and torn clothing so he went to each bathroom, knocked, and entered asking them if we could wash their clothes. He came back with an armful of them.

Why don't you put them in the wash, I suggested, since I'm not sure they'd want me in their private things.

He agreed and soon the water churning hum of the machine reached the sizzling on the top of the stove; the music of the day had begun. Silence to music or the music in silence. And this music of silence was part of what drew them back to us.

As we sat at the table, we knew they would stay. Henry would take the lead more with Michael, he would do so nonverbally yet surely. Michael relinquished the control and yet stayed articulate.

We washed and bandaged his hand. We went to the pharmacy for more supplies. They were there when we returned. We set up a table and two futons in the loft. It was a general transition. There were jobs they were able to maintain here and there with enough money from them so they could buy two bicycles.

THE EPISODE

When the song came, and it was not about being sonorous. It was like a clanging bell, ringing for the midwife to assemble and revise. One wanted to stop that tongue since she had heard enough of it. She wished. She wished she could place her hard hand on the metallic rust and just stop it, hold it, tell it that its job was over; it could rest, it could go into the well-deserved silent retreat.

Stopping tongue. And what underlies this tongue? The desire to group the young women, organize and enforce them, their forceps, their longing arms for the blood and mucus of new life ambivalently proceeding ever painfully entranced. And when they have that babe outside finally after eons of screams and please, where do they do first? Well to the tongue of course - taking out all that would still it, here a tongue not allowed to stop.

And that tongue will speak millions of words some true many fabricated to a will foreign yet familiar to its owner, its seeming origin. And that tongue first rigidly will let through the screams of the encounter with air, of nitrogen and oxygen and carbon dioxide, of atmospheres where longing, hope and despair cannot, will not, be distinguished.

And that tongue will lick and suck the white fluids immediately recognized and welcome. The feeling of pressure mid tongue, the pleasure of such pressure almost as enjoyable as the nutrient itself.

How many gallons of it even before the first word to which the tongue will contribute, will make it happen? This tongue does not care about the praises, the exhilarating exclamations, ejaculations of joy, of grief, coming from those on the outside. It is just for it: another movement, another exercise of pressure out of a desire for what is need.

Kneaded, as the skin of the infant is caressed and adroitly tapped as if the old typewriter, as if the adult is writing something on the very skin. Not the onion skin paper in the olden days, this skin is hardier and can take the sentences not caring if mistake or not.

It is a time before the tongue can itself tap out what the skin wants to say to who intrudes, who means well perhaps but the text is too long and misunderstood. It always comes to that point, that disjunction between tongue and skin. Tongue *wants* to report on skin's experience but there are the interruptions, the interventions again seemingly benevolent but stealing the desire including that to move the very tongue.

In this climate, the boy had an episode. It may have looked like a tantrum from the outside but it more was like a row of perfectly aligned, elaborately decorated porcelain cups crashing to the floor. Who knows why - perhaps an extraordinary wind that day, perhaps a juggling of the earth's hidden fault lines, perhaps the silent screams of a mother too embedded in her angst also that of the mother line.

So, the boy's episode was like the splintering of porcelain cups, about eight of them. The maid looked in, she had never once felt any fear of this boy but this day, this moment of the episode, she did. She tidied her cap. She straightened her apron, she looked again. She was standing just outside the door, peaking into the room of the episode.

It ended almost as quickly as it had begun so the maid did not have time to get help which, of course, was the idea that sprang to her mind immediately. The boy was sitting on the floor with his back to the antique cabinet, the shelf of which still contained, sitting upright as ever, the eight porcelain cups.

Had it even occurred, this episode, or not? The maid rubbed her eyes but not too hard since she really did not want any aftereffects. She went with carefully measured steps over to the boy. She checked if his eyes were clear and oriented or whether they registered the episode, as eyes will, by rather going in separate directions and looking dim.

The maid bent to the boy and looked into his eyes, squarely, without incident. What was that? Are you alright? Yes, Mimi, he replied, I was going to the kitchen to get a drink and then, here, it happened. Just like that. Did you see? I felt it more than I saw it, Mimi told the boy who was looking into her eyes with an apologetic plea.

Nothing to be sorry for lad, she told him. And then, instantly, she knew that was not the right tone, nor the right intent. She had to move out of her everyday maid self for her now to speak with, be with this boy. The episode had secured such. So, who was this after-episode boy with whom the maid was to be connecting, contacting, and relating to now? That was the question. But she was there and there was no time for such examination, she just went to where he was and that engendered a new sort of maid.

This after-episode Mimi then said: I did not mean what I just said. You look sorry for it, the episode. Why is that? You did not mean for it to happen. But, the boy countered, it did happen, and I am the person it happened to. It was me. It was more, she replied, that it went through you. No Mimi, it was me, the boy was shaking his head no, back and forth, rather quickly. Mimi wanted to cry in this after-episode place. She never had wanted to do so before with the boy.

She wiped her right hand across her apron as if she was removing some remnant of sweet potato pie in the process of its being neatly assembled. She put her hand up to the boy's cheek. She examined it: her hand on his trembling cheek, the cheek ready to receive a stream of tears if that was to be. The boy did cry, he cried right into her hand. She cupped his face with both her palms and gathered his tears, this outpour of shame and fear and grief. For, in the episode, the boy had entered a no-man's-land, that abyss, that negative capability, that cloud of unknowing and so in coming back from it, there was the perennial knot of shame, fear and grief, now releasing.

Don't tell anyone Mimi, please, don't say a word of it. She assured him that she would not. Come, she then said, let's get something to drink, a warm tea, and I'll put that special honey in it, the one we got from the farm, the one you like so much. So, the maid was the one who helped to bring the boy back. What if she had not been there? What if he came out of the episode and only a silent empty room greeted him with sparkling hints of the presence of ancestors long expired?

He may have panicked. He may have lost his breath in the sharp fear that marks the event as necessary to be put behind, cast out, and even more: eradicated completely. He most certainly would have tried to make it never-happened. He would have walked into the kitchen and gotten the drink still trembling as he was persuading himself that it had never occurred.

So, it would have stayed in the back-regions this journey to the abyss, since it never can be eradicated. It would stay so far away from his everyday life and consciousness that it would sleep until it woke not able to stay away any longer, having developed too much pressure from being pushed away, it would burst out, crashing through the boy's, his parents,' his great parents' defense systems. For no one, not even one of the past, even in 1400 AD or so in an impenetrable medieval castle, could keep the episode sleeping forever, thinking it eradicated.

And when it did burst through in any age, particularly if the person was an adult with a tremendous amount of power, it easily could be transferred to a war. Somewhere even the boy knew and now experienced that humans wanted anything but being in and with such an episode, seemingly groundless, asking its desire. Tongues won't report such episodes that are the skin's and beneath-the-skin's experience. So, the episodes accumulate silently and then suddenly burst out upon others.

So, the maid and the boy were having tea in the kitchen, tea with the special honey. The mother came in from her nap upstairs. She said she had a strange, difficult dream but that's all she said, for when it comes in dreams, it is most easy to push aside since like dew the dreams evaporate quickly at the first natural light though stay in their own non-temporal light. The mother took a cup of tea as well but, unlike other such afternoon teas, they all sat quietly for at least two minutes.

There are awkward silences and there are knowing silences and fortunately this was the latter. On what levels the three were communicating in these two minutes, that remains unknown. But what was known by them all was that they were communicating. It was about the episode. It was about its source and its effect. It mainly was questioning it though they all knew that it had happened.

The boy tapped his finger on his teacup and said clearly, yet without any trace of malice: I don't belong here. The eyebrows of the other two lifted in synchrony. I need to go out and be with friends my own age. I need air and sun.

The maid and the mother nodded simultaneously realizing that there was an excess of estrogen in the room, knowing that the boy was merging to the secret pain of this home as

well as all those homes of their family leading up to and included within it.

The shingles on the home were not surprised when he
emerged. They had been waiting for such a delivery for some
time, from his father, even from his grandfather. Both of the
latter two had gone into businesses which they had very far
from the home, so when the episodes were coming through,
they personally did not register or acknowledge them, but
instead their tongues let them become the warfare of the
workplace, of the marketplace, of the church, and of the political arena.

The shingles knew things. They wanted to tap the boy on his
shoulder and have him turn around and to say to him: It's
not that the maid and the mother in there are the problem
or too excessive or dangerous. That mis-vision must end
now. It's that you are tempted to hide within them and avert
their reality, letting it pass through you and not be connected
to your tongue, so it turns into outer conflict and woe.

It was as if the boy heard them, these shingles that so long
protected the family from the elements and strategies of pi-
rates penetrating privacies. For the boy did turn around. The
strange thing is that the episode, and the way the boy did
carry it, made him open to what was closed before, shingled

down now became shingles speaking. Call it old time wisdom, call it memory, or just listen. They may have been cracked, they may have been splintered and certainly they had caked-in crevices of their being that never would know light, but they had seen and now they spoke.

They spoke of flourishing, of the possibilities of a family enlarged to the possibility of not treading on each other and not bringing their conflict to the soul of the world. The fathers and the mothers spoke through the shingles. How could a boy called Ross understand such thing? Perhaps he did not. Perhaps it was enough that he just turned around and listened to them, these mud-caked splintered carriers of images and sounds striving to get through for possibly ages.

He was young but what he heard was: Don't let the episode go, don't think it did not happen and push it back to the abyss. Then it will simmer and emerge when least expected, in your dealings with others young and old, tarnished and innocent. So, he was turned around speaking to the shingles. He told them he wanted to run and hide but he knew he would get stuck, caught in blind repetitions preventing all school.

But to take the episode out? Yes, take it out, they advised. Ross went over and touched one shingle; it was warm, almost hot to his hand. I want to believe you, he said to one of the shingles. I want to understand. But also, I want to go out and just be a boy, play and compete and laugh with others my age, only my age.

That is one version of the story, the shingle responded, and it has been done again and again, but there are others. Ross let his hand slide off the shingle and into his pocket. The small pocketknife there was a strange comfort. He lifted it out and showed it to the shingle. I am a regular boy, I have my tools and toys and I want to fit in with the others, fit in mightingly. I want nothing of episodes and family carriages.

Understood, the shingle replied. And, Ross continued, I can use this knife to hurt you if you keep talking about the episode. It never happened, hear me? It never happened, he said again. The shingle remained calm and replied: That's what you say but you know it is not true. Ross opened his knife, he looked at the blade and he could see one of his eyes in the blade's reflection. It looked sad.

So, Ross closed the blade into the knife again. He took a deep breath, but it remained shallow. He had said 'mightingly.' It was not even a word, but he had said it and he knew what he meant. But he actually felt little, and his knife looked little, and his eye was sad. He did not say another word, but he turned from the house and walked away while he took out his phone to call his friends.

The maid had been watching him from the window. She barely had half of her face over the glass since she knew that Ross was in a vulnerable state, and she did not want to intrude in a way that would throw him further. She was mumbling, perhaps to her dead mother, perhaps a prayer to whom she did not know, asking for the knowledge to know how to be with the boy, this repository of ancient difficulty and persistent pathos.

Then he was on the phone and gone around the corner and she went back into the room wondering what to do at this time of such reflection, even deep meditation, what household task could be up to it? Any actually, she realized. All household tasks, circular and quiet and rhythmic, could meet her level of wonder and perturbation. She picked up her duster. No spray necessary today.

And Ross was on the phone; he reached two friends. They were hanging out they said. Like dried meat, he thought, but he went to them, and he hung out and was bored and discouraged. One had matches. Another had cigarettes or maybe what looked like cigarettes filled with some drug that could go more to head than lung. They asked for his pocket-knife to cut the tissue thin paper to make more of them. He gave it to them and never asked for it back. They offered him a hit, he declined. He was in a place already not ordinary, but he did not tell them that.

His phone was ringing. He was with his friends who were smoking. There was a corner nearby. Some woods meeting the town square made a corner with it. He said to his friends that he had to go, and, for no reason of which he was aware, he walked to the corner. There were two ways to go then.

His friends were in another direction at this point. They were laughing and smacking their lips, smacking their thighs with laughter. It was the sort of moment for them that would come back many years later at their high school reunion when, all suited businessmen each, they would stand in the same group, drinking and laughing and remembering who they were then.

Ross looked to the left across the square. It had walkways that crisscrossed to make easy access to each end point. Those walkways once were a way for people to meet and engage one another while walking, but it was not that sort of town now. Everyone now walked in a singular way and hardly noticed those about to pass. Not for me, Ross said, yet the woods to the right were not exactly welcoming either. There everything seemed interconnected, everything penetrated.

This sort of dilemma would mark his life: singular or meshed. Some say it was 'written' - these sorts of themes and decisions that would repeat over and over in barely disguised form. It definitely was a template of sorts. Such were the thoughts that would occupy him later, now there was a decision to make in the here and now, right now.

What if neither square nor wood? He looked to the walkway that allowed square and wood to meet. It was one he never had gone on. Did the episode require this be the way now? Was the episode the author of this decision? He just felt the impulse or, more, a prompting, something too he would understand much later.

The walkway was easy enough. A soft sidewalk, not the hardened and aged cement of the city. A soft walk that had been the first man-made surface the wizened women healers of old would encounter when they dared to step out of the woods, out of their territory at the outskirts. Ross wasn't thinking of such healers though he was closer to their outpost, their exile, than he knew at the time.

He began to walk more slowly. The houses were still grand yet spaced further apart as he proceeded. The tiny flowers and weeds at the edge of the walk became more bountiful. More wild buds, fewer homes. Yet it was as if he could hear the children playing in those homes, caught in their own unique fantasies and reveling in what they thought more assuredly was pretend.

Dogs barked from these homes as he passed. He was not perturbed by them, they were doing their work, appointed and
not, of protecting. As he hummed the tune he was making
up on the spot, he picked up a twig and whittled it with his
thumbnail as he walked. He could almost feel the dog he
would have, such a dog not allowed in his home due to loose
hair and mud and other releases uncomely and feared by the
adults.

When he got tired, he sat on the edge of the walkway and he
looked back, wondering how far he was from his home. It
was not a missing exactly, but it was a worry of how they
would worry. It was as if a huge elastic band was pulling him
back, but he knew he had a choice. He thought of the shingle
and in his mind he reminded his fathers and mothers that he
had to not throw away or erase the episode and he also had
to do that for them as much as for himself.

He looked down at his shoes. They were not the sort that one
would take on such a walk, but they were leather and hearty.
They were not going to interfere in whatever he decided. His
socks were dusty, the sand in their ribs reminding him of the
mud in the creases of the shingles. As the shingles again appeared to him, he remembered their teaching not to let go of
the episode.

Was the episode with him now? He asked himself. Was he running from it or was it that which was propelling him further? There was no one around. He was alone or felt very much so. No one to answer these questions, guide him through it, or so he thought.

As he thought about where to go, how to proceed and whether to continue on this walkway aligning wood, aligning square, he thought of not having a guide. He asked for one. He remembered the shingle and spoke to the fathers and mothers and said they had brought him to this point, and he needed a guide to go to where they had not.

The houses now were beginning to get smaller, in fact, almost looked like cottages. They were appealing even beckoning, their exteriors were not adobe exactly yet looked porous and as if they once had been soft and pliable. Their shutters had designs in them: a tree, a rabbit, a flower. The front doors were painted different colors, yet none thwarting. He almost wanted to stop at one for a cup of tea, a chat, a superficial introduction to pull him through another mile or so.

But he did not stop, and it was not in such a cottage that she found him. It was in the store ahead. It was just a common market: the sort to make the rich people feel like they were getting back to nature and yet also was just somewhat too expensive for the cottage people. But he was thirsty by now and he had a few coins on him. The drink was a red color that looked too transparent to be healthy, but he didn't care since the dehydration was spreading through him.

He deposited the bottle in the bucket for recycle and was heading towards the door when she spotted him. By the time the empty bottle clinked its landing, she was in front of him. She had on sandals that spoke a disinterest in the latest style, as did her dress, her hair, her simple, unpretentious stance. She was someone he would not have noticed if he passed her on the street, and he certainly did not notice her in the store before she was right up to him.

Do you need something, are you lost? These were her first words to him.

No, he backed off slowly.

You look tired, she said slowly with a calm that moved through him.

You have no idea, he answered. He didn't mean to say that but the words were out of him before he could trap them.

So, you are running?

He looked down, his shoes were quite dust covered and so looked worn out, as worn out as he felt and as she had surmised he was.

Do you miss your mother? She asked this slowly and quietly.

It's not that, I was too much their relief, their carrier.

He didn't mean ever again to refer to the episode but there it was.

I understand, she said, come with me.

Of course, he had been taught, drilled really, about strangers, not speaking with them, not going off with them, the vital dangers of such. But he was on a strange yet familiar road and he was alone and he knew he needed a guide. That knowledge, that ability to know he could not be alone with it all was his advantage; he also was to learn that many years later.

Therefore, he trusted her though he wasn't sure why except that it had to do with how she was so unassuming and unadorned. Of course, she could be dangerous or take him to those who were. But he had to trust or leave, and he decided to trust.

She took his arm and led him out the door. The sun had the brilliant direct rays indicating its setting was in motion. These rays cut into his eyes in their contrast with the shadows in the store. His eyes teared up. He knew the import of the moment and that also contributed to the tears. But as soon as the tears arrived, they were gone, brushed away by the soothing breeze that said it's OK, go on.

It was all a bit dizzying: the episode, the leave-taking, the meeting, the decision, the walking out of the dimming market into these striking, slanting rays. He thought perhaps he was tottering, but also he knew that she still had his arm. They passed a police station and a fire station. They must be at the center of some town, some little town more like a village.

She was, one could say, ordinary looking. Her brown hair was not highlighted, her wrists and fingers had no bands or rings. Her gaze and speech were all that of an educated, though not over-educated, person of that time. There was an atmosphere in her voice however, misty without being nebulous. It spoke of another sphere, another form of life.

She saw him observing her and she gave him a ribbon that she took out of a pocket. It was blue satin and worn, wrinkled, a kind of blue that settles the stomach, the kind of blue of spiritual kinship.

She definitely was a daughter, he felt that immediately. It was not that he was taking the arm of a figurative mother, or an aunt or a grandmother. She was the sort of person who, when thinking of herself, would say: I am Cecilia, daughter of Petra. So, as he had taken her arm, he took the gift of her ribbon, putting it in his right pocket.

Tempted as he was to ask: What does this mean, all of this? - he did not. That was a particular quality he had, a distinguishing one, and one inherited through the family line: he could proceed step by step yet without servitude and with a curiosity not being piercing. So, Ross and Cecilia walked down the road on which he had begun, on which he had run into her when he had asked for a guide.

It was not that he expected bears in the forest or dangerous animals of any sort, but he preferred not to look to the right at that wood. At times, a particularly friendly or aesthetic home to the left would catch his eye, but for the most part he looked straight ahead. Sometimes she fiddled with her left hand and that would catch his eye as well. Were there personal bonds she had? He decided not to wonder or ask.

They came to a point in the road where the homes got even further and further apart and soon there was mainly land, uncultivated, in front of them. Here and there was someone's farm from the olden days going its own way. Indeed, they saw the ruin of a barn further up. This was when she decided that they would get off the road which had well served them and had been the beginning of their time together.

So, they sat in the ruin of the barn and she asked about his parents: Would they not be concerned with his absence? Would they not worry? Of course, his nod replied. So, you will be brought out of time, she said. It will only be one-half hour by the time you return home, and they won't know you were away this far, they will think it only a time that you were with your friends.

So, you are a friend? he asked.

Of course, the reply.

And you can move outside of time?

We can both be brought outside of this time, yes.

Let's do so.

You are not afraid at all?

I had an episode, and I don't want to have more back there.

Good that you know you can't flee from such things. We're going to a place that episodes go. Yet, she continued, now you are not alone, and I know the place well.

There is nothing more to say, he thought it first and then said it by getting up.

So, she took a piece of board that had fallen, that once was part of the wall of a grand barn housing many purebred horses and some random birds. She remembered the board that her friend had tripped over that allowed descent into the memory of the loved one. So, Cecilia broke the plank carefully on her left knee and she looked into the frayed edge of one piece and then the other. She took his hand and together they stepped into the space between the two splits.

Ross thought it would be a tunnel but it was not. He had read the fairy tales. He had spun further tales on his own as a child sitting in the toy room surrounded by possibilities of fantasy lands and adventures there. Others, even you, may think it would be a staircase that they descended leading to the archetypal remains of old cellars.

He shut his eyes, he took her hand, glad there were no rings to cut into him in this penetration into abyss. He had no time to reach for the ribbon in his right pocket but he thought of it, it was in his inner mind as the two of them proceeded in what felt like going step by step yet actually was more a plunge of sorts. Others might think there would be mists to tear through in a swimming motion, or a membrane that only a certain propulsion could tear through.

Instead he smelled a particular scent like the one his grandmother, the one born into a family not rich, not elegant like that of the other grandmother, yet more of a simple life, the scent that that one would wear. He always had liked it, in fact, he kept her bottle of it when she had died, as a commemoration, smelling it whenever he missed her or had a particularly vivid memory of their time together.

The scent calmed him enough so he could open his eyes. He saw that they still were walking on level ground but instead of the rural land with homes and a few centers, there was a pinkish ground with trees of a clear viridian green. The outreach of their branches suggested plums, the sort of purple with specks of red. Yes, indeed, he looked up, they were plums, and they were reaching out to him.

Cecilia noticed. She said that he should not touch anything and certainly not eat anything. What is this place called? he asked. Carnation, she answered. They walked further on and there, on the right, the tree had cherries, no plums, cherries looking like they were exhibiting themselves in a dance or like happy chatty folks at a casual party outdoors.

He really did want to try one of those cherries, but one glance in her direction impelled him otherwise. She looks older, he noted, was there not now some gray in her hair? Were the eager wrinkles around eyes that smiled been there before? Even her hand felt heavier in his, like it had been through more than she had bargained for. He felt the stupor come on quickly. Oh, to lay at the base of one of these trunks, to cuddle by it and dream.

That was the old way, staying hooked into the mother, you are closer to yourself now, she whispered into his ear that did not want yet to hear that. And, as she finished the word "way," the ground softened, he felt it beneath both soles, it became more malleable, collecting footprints whereas before it had not.

The stupor was coming across him heavily now and he just wanted to lie down. His gait slowed; he was falling behind her though their hands still held. She stopped, turned, and looked into his eyes. It's your choice, of course, but you know if you sleep and go back you continually will have to run from and thus repeat the episode, all of it.

As she spoke, he was wishing he had bought some substantial food in that market back there, since he was realizing a great hunger. Between the stupor covering him and the hunger, he really did not feel that he could go on. He began to sit, she caught him from the back, both her arms beneath his armpits. He felt the tears begin to come from behind his eyes.

Don't wish or wipe them away, she told him. They are a crucial aspect of our entry here. They know more than you do right now about how to proceed. Please Ross, let them through. So, he did. Many of them. He felt them come at first from behind his eyes, then from behind his tongue, then from his throat and then, suddenly from the pit in his stomach, the pit that he had misjudged as hunger. These tears were his as well as those of his family line; they wanted so much from him: his attention to an opening that felt ominous and irrevocable. No one in his family had risked it before. Of this he was sure, of this he already knew. She gave him tissue so soft yet, paradoxically, not tearing or crumbling when wet.

Or maybe, since it was so soft and satiny, it was not tissue yet the antique handkerchief from the other grandmother; tissue or handkerchief, it did its due. It collected what seemed a reservoir. He recalled often driving past one, a reservoir, his mother at the wheel when they were returning from the city. He would look out of the window at it. Perhaps he had had then a premonition of the surplus of his family's suffering, uncollected, not seen, put aside for future generations, for him.

Now the reservoir was moving through him. Am I only to be a channel for this generation? Am I like a straw for that which was unheeded, ignored, attempted to be erased to now charge through? Am I to live as a straw? But such questions only melted into the water washing through him, and, in fact, washing him. Call it a purification of him; call it a purification of the ancestors. Can a boy need such? Certainly, it was not only the family's need, though it was that. It was also for him.

So, he did not sit down, he did not reach for or eat the cherries, he did not cuddle at the base of any trunk. He still had her hand and that amazed him. When he settled into the tears, it all came easier. He almost relaxed and then they were through, they were over. He was tired but no longer hungry, and he no longer had a need to sit or to sleep.

Then her hand on his felt clammy and it was time to let that go also. So, you see, she said, I won't be a substitute for the house with mother, with maid. It is not a return to them through me, though they as the base are secure and they are the anchor allowing us to go on.

So, they did go on. We resemble something, he said.

What do you mean?

I bet from someone looking at us from the outside, we resemble something.

What might that be?

A brother and an older sister who are exploring.

I can see that though I know where to go.

Thank you, he said somewhat meekly and with relief.

Then he saw what looked like a canyon upside down on the ground. It had to be some sort of a structure or a building he thought yet to him it looked like an upside-down canyon.

Its surface was the mud of ages, dried, soggy, dried again, hardening yet again over the years and centuries collecting very small pockets of air in its substance. So, it was hard, very much hardened and porous simultaneously.

We're supposed to go in there? He asked cautiously.

Scary from the outside?

It's an upside-down canyon or a humungous beehive that became hard and stuck. I do not want to get stuck.

That's always the fear, she said. You are not at all unusual to worry such. Let's walk alongside it first.

It was so large that they could not possibly circle it, not with their tiredness that more and more was edging in upon them and not even without the tiredness for the structure was that large. It looked like it wanted something, and Ross decided immediately that that something would not be him.

So, he pulled away from her for the first time since they had met. He stood aside and looked up - he hardly could see the top of it when that close to it; it was that large.

So, this is the land of Carnation.

This is part of it, one could say, part of the entrance to it.

I'm not going in.

Well, let's climb it so you can get to know it.

Climb it? Are you serious? I'm ready to go home rather do that. They're missing me for sure.

They won't know you're gone. In this land, your time is stopped.

Well, I'm missing them, I can't climb this thing. We'll never get to the top, we'll never get to the other side. As he said this, he began to slump, and he knew instinctively that was not good.

It's not about climbing it to the top, she said, trust me, you've trusted me this far. If you go back now, there only will be more episodes when least expected and to the benefit of no one. After the tears of so many in and through you, there is a burial and then there are ways to remember in peace, to keep in memory and honor that which is buried. That is what this is.

All right, he said, and he stood up and for the first time he looked at her eye to eye.

Then at that moment it was just him. She was there but, in his head, heart, blood stream, nerves, muscles, organs and bones. He looked ahead at the great mass. It was a tan color with tinges of ochre. He began the climb. About a half a mile up, he saw an entrance. It was a small cave. He remembered his lessons. David with Saul and David just taking the bit of the hem. Who will forgive him this?

He went into the cave. His heart registered his anxiety, but Cecilia was in there urging him on, calming him, ebbing and flowing like the sea, she was there as he went step by step carefully placing toe first, hands outstretched. He blinked to familiarize himself with the dark. He licked his lips which were drying as his panic mounted. This panic and Cecilia were dialoging in his very being when he saw her: a small girl huddled and what looked like whitish stone rubble around her. She was more afraid of him than he was of her.

He asked: What is your name? She looked at him without replying. She was shivering. He realized that she might not have his language. So, he put out both arms, opening palms up to her to show that he was not offending yet offering. He stopped moving so she could get used to his smell, his bearing, his own fear.

They stayed quiet for some time. Yet he could sense the truth of Cecilia's words that there was no chronological time here. He approached the girl slowly. She put her head between her knees, shaking now more evidently. He placed his right palm carefully on her back, held it there, calming himself so only peace would be transferred.

When she looked up, he saw streaks of dirt on her face and tears in her eyes. She had been escaping from someone or something. He looked into those eyes and told her he would help her, he was not afraid of the place or of her. He said that he always had been afraid of her and that his entire family had been afraid of her. That in evading, running from or trying to destroy her, they had lived shallow lives and created much suffering for others. She looked at him with a curious look indicating that she did not understand his language.

He thought of Cecilia. Of course, Cecilia knew all of it: she knew this girl, and she knew that he finally was going to find her. We have to get out of here, he said. He went to her and, with his hand on her back, helped her up and walked slowly with her to the mouth of the cave. But what to do next was the question, he wasn't sure he could maneuver the wall with her this way, the side of the upside-down canyon.

He knelt down and motioned for her to hold onto his back. He was surprised and relieved that she did so. As she was touching his back, he felt the pain of many in his family, coming as shock waves, crashing, inflating to crush all in their stead.

This pain crippled him with its waves of rage and sorrow. He crouched down. He knew he never could scale down the wall with her with these cycles of terrifying pain. He went back into the cave and sat down with her still at his back. She still was holding onto his shoulders. He hoped that the pain would begin to subside and feared it would increase, yet neither occurred.

Here was just the steady pouring of it. He sought Cecilia; he
went deeply within to find her. He found her within his pel-
vis and, when he went to her, she was sitting watching the
huge storm waves pounding the shore a quarter of a mile
away.

He approached her slowly, he still had the girl holding onto
his shoulders. Already Cecilia knew he was there, she smiled,
her face looked translucent, and she opened her palms to
him.

I've been expecting you Ross, I am so pleased you found her.

We found her, he replied, you are always with me now.

But you made your way alone and that's admirable, for a boy
to finally accept her.

I'm more than a boy, I'm thirteen. Who is she? What is her
name? What am I supposed to do with her?

She will tell you, show you.

But how the heck do I get her down that mass of reversed
canyon?

Accept the pain waves, hear them, acknowledge.

And then?

They will carry you.

When she said that, she was gone, and Ross was still sitting in the cave with the girl holding onto his shoulders. He felt the next wave. It mounted and was about to crash into him, he felt pain in every nerve, racking his soul. He acknowledged it, he felt what had been a betrayal. It was between siblings; it was violent, and it had repeated for a few generations.

Now will you stop? He asked one of the brothers caught in the wave. Will you recede, will you let it go? And what is it that you want me to see in it?

I want you to see how it still lives in you as it did your uncle.

I don't have siblings like he did.

You would direct it at someone you love who is similar to you.

Why the raw edge of this cutting over and over? Ross asked, continuing: Why don't you forgive him and yourself? Where is forgiveness, where is compassion? Again: Why the raw edge of this cutting over and over?

Forgiveness won't happen without repetition until you acknowledge the pain as you are and compassionately receive us as you are.

Then the next wave crashed upon him. It was about repeated adulteries and how the ones betrayed felt. He attended to it as he located and spoke to a wife. As he did so, he could ride the wave and not get pummeled by it.

And this adultery pain spoken by the wife and acknowledged in compassion by Ross, heard in the very fiber of his being, carried him with the girl holding onto his shoulders out of the mouth of the cave. The next wave contained substance abuse and the domestic violence associated with it. He was speaking with a man who was old, haggard, and in despair. He remembered him in the family tree, now he saw and spoke to him.

The waves brought him and the girl to the bottom of the reversed canyon. At the base, he put her down and the waves of pain stopped as soon as she was off him. She looked at him with curiosity. She also looked like she had more energy; she was less debilitated and seemed lighter.

He let some minutes transpire while they rested and then he asked her name. She looked at him again curiously but with a clarity that was just starting to come to her eyes like something definite moving through a vast memory.

Anita.

It was so clear.

As was her next gesture: she pulled up her socks. They were off-white and ribbed. Her shoes were light walking shoes made of canvas. The dress she had on went to just below her knees and was tan cotton over a blue jersey.

She sat there looking at him. He said: I know you are wondering who I am and where we are going. I am Ross. I come from a home in another town. I had an episode. That was the summary of much pain in our family line that was not felt or understood or acknowledged and rightly buried over generations. And that is you, Anita.

But, of course, she knew that, and the question was how to get her home and what was her home. He knew he had to rightly bury and commemorate the waves which was to bring her home. We're going home, he told her. Can you walk? But she already was up by the time he finished the sentence.

So, he walked by her side on a sidewalk in a way that would lead but not dominate. The houses got less far apart as they

proceeded. He was amazed at Anita's strength and persever-
ance and how different she had become as he had experienced the waves of pain through generations.

He knew that he needed a drink of water, so they moved
from the sidewalk to the field and then to the edge of the
woods looking for a stream. He felt that he was too far from
the market to wait until then to hydrate.

But there was no stream anywhere in sight or smell. He asked
Anita if she could tell if there was water anywhere, but she
nodded no, and he realized that she was not very much familiar with this world or its resources yet also that she was
not frightened. We'll have to ask, he said.

So, they walked back to the sidewalk and approached the first
house they saw. It was neither grand nor poor but could use
some repair. The door was solid with no window or knocker.
He knocked with his knuckles. Anita looked patient and
knowing at his side.

Slowly the door opened, and someone looked out of the
crack. We are harmless, he said, we are returning home after
a journey and I'm very thirsty and am wondering if you
could be so kind to give us a drink of water.

There were no questions asked, no conversation. The cup was a yellow plastic, the sort one would have at a barbecue or an outside gathering. He smelled into it and it smelled like ordinary water. He took a sip and it tasted like water. Perhaps he should have gotten to know these people before accepting it. Perhaps he should have asked for their hose instead.

He left the water at the door, further untasted. He could not afford it: coming this far and being hurt by someone who wouldn't speak to him. Yet he really didn't think he had it in him to make it to the market. Meeting Cecilia, following her, the upside-down canyon, the cave experience, meeting Anita and the waves of pain, ironically waves of water, had taken all his energy and he was very dehydrated.

He walked a few steps back to the sidewalk with Anita and then he sat on the curb and called for Cecilia. She resonated deeply within him, and she sounded like she had been expecting him. Anita seemed to recognize Cecilia's voice because the young girl perked up and oriented to it. It came, this voice, as the drink of water for which he had thirsted.

But it was not enough. I am so very thirsty, he told Cecilia, I can hardly breathe, and my legs are weak and beginning to tremble. Just walk carefully, she said, as if you are in physical therapy with bars on each side that you push off of with your arms. Anita is fine, you are the thirsty one.

So, he stood up and imagined walking on a mat with two bars that he leaned into and that supported him as he pushed off, step by step. Anita slowed down to his pace. He thought she would be impatient, but she was not. In fact, she looked up to him, eye to eye, at her initiative, for the first time.

What a look! It said: This is right, go on, keep going. It was the look that every creative or adventurous one needed to proceed, whether it came from within, whether without. He walked slowly on the mat for the space of three houses which were getting closer together. Then there was a step that made the bars fly away in an instant. Upon what had he landed that caused the sudden change?

Anita still was by his side. He took her hand. He looked down - there was no mat, there was no equipment of any kind. He sat down and the tears came, a young man, a boy of thirteen, filled with tears. Just his own tears, not more from and through the family, just his own. He wept while Anita sat by his side. She did so in a way that assured him that "go on" also included this, sitting with his own personal pain.

The sky was changing as he sat. It went from cerulean blue to lemon yellow at the horizon. Some would say later that it was the first day of summer. Then the lemon yellow at the horizon reached out to them. It was a long ray, wide, almost a sidewalk width but translucent.

They both knew what they had to do. They stood up and stepped onto the lemon yellow that was now a walk. When their feet touched it, it felt like walking on pudding or a very, very soft mattress.

It is so soft this walk, yet it holds us, he said to Anita; at first, I thought we were going to go through it, fall through, but it holds us. Anita was sure-footed, she actually walked ahead of him a bit. Their hands fell to their sides, there was no need of holding onto one another now. Then he felt a great relaxation coming upon him, his shoulders softened, his neck muscles gave up trying to hold head and body both, his calves became more supple.

As they proceeded on the lemon-yellow walkway, it slanted up. Yet what they noticed was that paradoxically they did not have to exert more energy to compensate for this incline. It was as if it was simultaneously slanted and horizontal in terms of the energy it took for them to continue walking.

He thought of Mt. Everest. He thought of all the effort humans put into climbing. He thought of the saints, he thought of the astronauts, he thought of children building forts in the highest branches. He thought of how actually every climb also was horizontal. He kept going. He thought he saw what was the sun ahead, a small orange disc.

As they got closer to it, however, the disc did not change size. It stayed small; it did get warmer as they approached it but not hot enough for it to be a sun or part of a sun. Were they walking to a new planet? Cecilia, he asked, is this for me to live in a way that is new, on a new planet, to continue the family line in a way different from the old ways of running from the pain but in a new place? Are we going to a new planet to begin again?

No, she replied from the depth of his being, it is all part of returning to your family. You will live with them as someone who no longer has to repeat the running from the pain in ways that hurt or even torment lives. But this is a part of bringing Anita home and returning to them.

So, they kept walking to the orange disc. It was round after all. From a distance, it had looked like it could be a plate even though he thought it a new planet, it had looked more like a plate. But now they saw it three dimensionally. They felt themselves getting warmer as they approached yet suddenly, without notice, the lemon-yellow walkway became a shallow pool of water leading to the base of the orange disc. The water cooled them, felt energizing and, of course still thirsty, he wanted to drink it.

Go ahead, Cecilia advised, this is pure and nothing in it that would hurt or impede either of you in any way. So, then they each bent down and cupped their hands into it, quickly and repetitively lifting the water to their lips. As this was happening, each kept an eye on the orange disc to be sure that it didn't move.

Then there was no water any longer and the yellow of what had been the walkway merged into the orange disc. They were at it, at its front edge and, surprisingly, the temperature had not risen. They were not burned, not even over-heated, but it was just a simple, even warmth they had been experiencing since they first saw it.

Ross thought about appealing to Cecilia on how to proceed but then he knew to go right up to it to actually touch it, put his nose to the orange surface. Then the surface opened and they both were enveloped by a substance that felt like jelly. Anita clutched his hand, she said she could breathe in it and asked if he could breathe fine also. Yes, he said, let's keep going. Both were keeping their eyes shut.

The contact of their hands was warmer than the gel-like substance that was encompassing them. Ross opened one eye and saw that the gel did not go into his eye yet instead allowed vision through itself. It's fine to open our eyes, he said gently to Anita while exerting more pressure on her hand. Four eyes were now open and what was ahead looked like a Ferris wheel, it was circling but there was no one on it.

The man running it at the base of it said hello to them. Are we in a ghost town? Ross asked him. No, the children who were on here were circling in great pain until you found Anita and the waves hit you and now they are free. They are in the own scenarios being who they are meant to be. Anita spoke up then: So, why are you still running it? He chuckled and said: It's a way of releasing the energies of pain and lightening it up; the saints are riding on it now my lass and doing just that.

Ross and Anita stared now at the seats. They focused intently and squinted their eyes. No, I don't see them sir. The man suggested that they look up vertically first and ask for them and then look again at the seats. The two did so, and then together they both looked at the uppermost seat. There were two there, a male and a female. Their robes did not distinguish them but the golden circle above their heads did.

It was then that Anita heard them speaking and she and Ross looked at the Ferris wheel again and saw that each seat had two saints on it, a male and a female, all speaking to one another. What are they saying? Anita asked the man.

They each have a name, he said, and come from different parts of the world, different eras, different languages, different ways of being overall yet all are extraordinary and here with you now. I am not in charge here, he continued, and I do what's right to do.

Anita asked the man to stop the wheel and she looked inquisitively at the first couple who were now directly across from her. She reached out to them, not with her hand but with her heart speaking through her eyes. When she said the first words to them, the gel surrounding everything disappeared. Now there was air, now there was earth.

On firm land, breathing air, they looked up again and, for the first time, they noticed that one seat had only one sitting in it. It was a male with the same sort of robe on him and golden circle above him as the others. Anita and Ross looked at one another with a sharp twist of recognition and sorrow. It's for you, he said softly. Yes, I know, she replied, and I will be with you still. Ross pulled the blue ribbon from his right pocket and gave it to her.

She nodded to the man running the wheel and he lowered it so that the seat with the one male was in front of them. Anita got in. She and the male hugged one another. She looked to Ross and took his hand again. She kissed it and let it go. The wheel moved forward.

As it did so, the wheel, the saints, and the man at the base all disappeared. There was a sidewalk lining a simple road surrounded by middle class colonial type homes, white mostly, with fences surrounded by motley and beautiful assortments of flowers. Ross knew to keep walking. Cecilia, he called to her, do you know the saints?

Yes, we are all here, she replied. I've known them before their births. He then asked: Are you my guardian angel then? As he spoke, he noticed that a thread was inside connecting every part of his body to everywhere he had been during what would be registered as a half an hour. Yes, she replied, and you have known me since your birth. He said to her: You have helped me have my tongue be now inextricably bound to my skin and what is beneath my skin, so my tongue's words can be true, and I thank you so much; now let's go home. Yes, she replied.

But, of course, the boy who returned home after the registered half an hour was not at all the boy who had left. As if it was a scent they picked up, both his mother and Mimi sensed that immediately. He went into his room and shut the door to collect himself. It was not so much an issue of putting himself together, as if he were in pieces, but it was an absorbing of where he had been, what he had felt and what he had now in knowledge that he had not had before.

Later when his father returned from his office day and they were all sitting at the table at dinner, his father looked at him strangely. What happened today, son? The silence was not long but it rapidly reverberated. I saw things, Ross replied, I see the pain in the family line and the sacrifices needed to carry it. But we are being watched carefully now and the pain is protected finally.

Hmm, his parents said almost in unison. He was from then on more a stranger to them as he was more intimate with them than ever before. It was the same at school and later in his work. Though he helped others go to where he had been and to return, and though he had a way of being affable enough, he never fit in anywhere completely. In understanding such, it was something, strangely enough, he never regretted.

THE FORGOTTEN-ABOUT TOWN

Fourteen years seems like a long time ago if one is in our chronological time. But there are many times, and my story is of the Kairos time which our Pastor mentioned last Sunday. That is the moment in timelessness, when our time intersects with Eternity. Still, fourteen years seems like a long time ago.

The carriage drive had some gravel over its firm surface and that could be from any time I suppose. Did I see the gravel while walking towards the house, was it in a side glance? Or did I bend to it, struck by a particular whiteness in it? Did the heel of my shoe brush it off with no notice? Why am I telling you the story at all when I can brush it off as my heel had done with that gravel that hinted white to me?

I am not trying to woo you or cause you woe for that matter. Though the very denial of such points to my concern, of course. You are the best example of the good attender for this story, and you will see such at its close. I know you are responding to it as I write, I feel it and hear it in my heart and that is what makes you such a good attender.

So, I walked down the carriage drive. The carriage was not in sight, but I knew that the lady was home. The ribbons I had bought as a gift would be welcome, I was sure. She could use them for holding her needles or for the sashes at the window or even for the decorating of the hem of her dress. They were of various shades all of the varied blue.

I never was really afraid of her, yet I did think that the ribbons would be a calming of sort. There had been so many - how do I even describe it - so many of the rough edges between us.

But she opened the door with a smile and genuinely seemed pleased that I had brought her a gift. The bottom of her dress barely brushed the floor as she led me into her parlor. I noticed that it was still slightly dark this floor, still drying, as if her maid had scrubbed it earlier in the day. Was that for me? Was I to be, am I to be a formal guest after all in this large home?

She led me into the parlor which was furnished to the elegance. I said to her: Mrs. Whittaker, your parlor is mighty splendid. She replied that recently they had the chairs re-upholstered, and she had chosen the fabric with the bunches of pink roses surrounded by hunter green leaves on a tan background to match the walnut frame of each chair.

She sat on the less elegant chair. I guessed, given the past, that she did so to give the appearance of humility. I wondered then if true humility even could be measured and, as I was sitting in the more elegant chair, I had to cancel the thought that her "humility measurement" in actuality would be very low. The standing clock encased in the mahogany cabinet was on the mantle of the large, welcoming hearth.

She graciously received my gift of the ribbons. She told me that there were many ways she could use them though she did not tell me which. I noticed a slight tremble in her fingers as she wove the ribbons through them, and this surprised me. She always had been so steady and sure in every gesture and posture. Her posture was so straight it amazed me at some times.

She had been speaking continually since the moment I arrived and mainly it was criticizing people we both knew though I had been listening with only half of my attention while the other part looked over the place. Such roaming I did to check things was not new but had been a sort of protection, at least I thought as much, for most of my adult life.

So, this half of my attention scouted around the home as well as the room and came back more or less sure that there was no apparent danger to my wellbeing even given the difference in our position and heredity. But I knew that I could venture only so far this way through the home's crevices, what webs within those high veiled rafters, what scurrying within walls so long ago constructed. So, I put my eyes on her in front of me and here she was this woman and still speaking, still twining the new ribbon in slightly trembling fingers.

So, I focused on her speaking, on her mouth. I noticed small, tiny even, strain lines around it yet overall her face was not as revealing of the tension I knew it must have gathered over the years. She was telling me about her daughter, now living in another part of the state, recently married, and wanting a child. It was difficult for me to imagine this woman, sitting diagonally to me, as a grandmother.

She told me that her daughter had received a new sleigh as a wedding gift, and this made visits more probable. A tabby cat walked into the parlor with a sense of ownership and rubbed his side against the part of my hostess' dress that was trickling like a stream and resting on the floor near the hearth. Your tabby seems to have the positive affections for you, I said. She replied that he could be a nuisance but was good at getting the rats.

More words: her husband was in town getting a new harness for his main horse. Will I have tea? In came the housemaid

and a tray. The maid never looked up; the tray was bounti-
fully arranged which did not surprise me. As the tea was
poured, I noticed how the china pot was just so delicate and
such a difference to the mistress's almost pointed nature.

It was not her words themselves but the way they were spoken, their aim, their direction into me. We are sure enjoying
the preparations of the Thanksgiving gathering coming up, I
said. She replied that they might go to it, but it was not so
important to them.

Her left foot abruptly moved to the left outside her skirt and
it seemed as though the movement was involuntary. Her
shoe was well worn but of a thin leather with a feminine cast
and once must have been expensive. I noticed how nervous
she was beneath her seeming to feel so sure of herself.

She began speaking of two families in town and how they
had taken to battling. She went into darkened details of how
a squabble became the battle and I sat there taking in the
negatives she portrayed of people I had known to be struggling and doing their best.

We were thus engaged in speaking about our daily life as I
wondered about this difference between the underflow of
her nervousness and her appearance of being in charge of
everything and superior to others. I stood and picked up the

ball of yarn that had dropped off the small, claw-foot table next to her as she reached for her tea. The yarn was a sallow yellow, not very attractive and almost the color of the very nervousness heretofore examined. I rummaged through all the ways I might use such a color but found none appealing.

She was collecting the teacups; she was moving to the kitchen. I followed like an obedient dog. I saw onions and carrots on the cutting block and remnants of chicken feathers. I was surprised that she would take me into this more private room. I wondered who would play music later after dinner. Who on the piano? Who on the flute? What pleasant sounds filling the atmosphere of the then filled stomachs would attempt to counter that sharpness coming from the underlying nervousness, that sallow yellow?

She was ushering me out now. The maid was nowhere in sight, but I heard what sounded like the beating of rugs outside. I left thinking of how very little was accomplished in this visit if such could be measured by a contact that seemed aligned with one's purpose in life. Goodbye and thank you for receiving me this day, I said on leaving. Don't trip on the walk, she replied as she shut the door.

Instead of taking the road home, I walked in the direction of the hills. They were slow sloping and had occasional heather breaking up the sameness of brownish green. But mostly they were round and soft, welcoming with no opposite motion of anxiety and authority. They knew who they were, and they just were without any speaking to impose about their own worth.

The wind had a sound to it but was without enough force to halt my motion into this welcoming terrain. It was like entering a soft reception that also was actively working on me and what I had to offer. For these were not passive hills, not dead, nor unfeeling for sure.

I went halfway up one and sat. There was enough dried grass to make the seat itch, yet I refrained from judging it. Here there was no sense in claiming any sense of my power. Being with my hostess there had been no choice: she had to have the power or there would be a hidden and possibly dangerous struggle. Yet did my being human on this hill just assert a power automatically? I relaxed into the hill. It was just there, supporting without being something lower than me and it offered me a peace that was as needed as it was unfamiliar.

A bird overhead squawked, it seemed happy to be going south. I let go of my responsibilities. It was a slow unravelling. They went along with the bird for a time until they came back to me again as they will.

I lay down and put my face in the crook of my arm. I lent myself more to the hill and to just lie with it all in this very peace. I asked the hill what it wanted of me in exchange. It didn't flinch, there was no tremor within it. Instead, it seemed in my imagination to grow around me more, so I was more encased as if it was a large earth-well saturated with water surrounding me: just this soft, fluid earth covered with green tendrils here and there that had their own sustenance and did not need mine to flourish or even be.

That is when I would have heard the child's voice in the past but there wasn't even that. My hostess of a couple of hours ago was far from my thoughts except once when I thought that she most likely was overseeing the stuffing of the chicken, the placement of her pretty pewter dinner plates.

Surrounded by this hill emerging as wet earth fortifying me, I sat quietly until it became a thin wreath around my neck. How strange: it was made of leaves and dried flowers woven together with yarn and heavy thread. It may have been a prize from another time. I remembered my prizes in spelling at school, for the blueberry pie at the Church fair, for the knitted scarf at the county fair. I knew I had to remove the wreath. So, I took it off and put it at my feet. At that moment, the hill came back to its size and I was there out in the open, no earth-well, no wreath.

I understood, as I got up, that that was the exchange: the hill offered me a letting go of any ways I thought I was better than others. I never had flaunted such prizes of my worth outright but maybe without awareness I showed them as I went along in the world.

It was as I was walking on the road towards my home that I realized how my hostess that day was a copy of me. I opened myself to this idea with some fear. My carriage drive was not as broad or long as hers with its gravel tinged with white, yet I realized how the mirror was there: how I was my hostess just in that thought, in making that comparison. I realize how the mirror was there in how I secretly held my prizes as I went about.

Yet to step out of it: to learn from this mirror and then let go of all ways I held onto my prizes, my power, ways I did resemble her - would that not leave me open to beating and humiliation? The ones who could do that were called saints, but what about us little ones? The hostesses of the world were too big for us, their pain was covered over as power that was too much for us littler ones who had too much to lose if we let go of resembling them.

Back at our land, I got some water from the pump and washed my hands, drying them when I entered my home. There still were many tasks to be done that day: preparing the dinner, putting the horse and cows back in the barn as well as finishing the sewing and darning of the night before. I wondered about the happy birds I had seen flying south. There are so many ways to fly away from what I had been realizing this day.

We did not have enough money for a maid, but Matilda would come often and volunteer to help as a good friend, as a neighbor and as an angel who hardly knew her place on earth. She seemed to appear when I was under the most stress and there was too much to do. At Church, they would say that it was the Holy Spirit that brought her, and for that I was grateful.

She entered this day as if she never had been away. I offered her tea, but she declined and helped me scrape the vegetables for dinner. She had brought over a loaf of bread made that day for me as if she had seen my visit to the hostess and my troubled and then fortifying time in the hills afterwards.

After we put in the vegetables to boil, Matilda briefly took my hand and squeezed it asking about my time with Mrs. Whittaker. On the outside fine, I answered slowly, but I added that she as usual was in her prideful place. Her home did look splendid. But underneath she was a mess, like her carriage had lost a wheel and she was stranded: she was jittery and not at all in peace. She ate a lot too. How much is that my jealousy talking - well, I don't know, I admitted to Matilda - she did have some mighty splendid things in her home and the two maids to do everything for her.

Matilda nodded. She was helping me do some darning at this point. I noticed that she had looked a bit tired the minute she arrived, but, strangely, now she looked refreshed and pretty again. The helping others revives her, I thought, and that's because she's good not because she needs to be on top. The thing about her is that she never is interested in gossip like the rest of us in this place. That means, I thought, she's not so empty to need it like the rest, including, too many times, myself.

For I did want to continue with the negative on Mrs. Whittaker. It was like it seemed to be more important than those vegetables to my wellbeing. Giving up the wreath on the hill seemed to make me hungrier.

I need the pastor to come and speak to me about the hunger. I said this suddenly to Matilda - interrupting the flow of our talk - because I really want to go on gossiping about that woman. She annoys me so.

Honest of you, Matilda said thoughtfully.

What keeps you so full that you don't need this tainted sugar candy to eat? I asked her. The question came out automatically and hit the mark.

Yes, it's always security at root, she replied.

What? We each have security. I have a house and Mrs. Whittaker has much more.

A different security, she replied - yes, things, objects, help of course but are not enough - it's the security of being recognized as if it was by someone who knew you your entire life.

Like a grandmother or aunt or who? The souls with God above?

Yes, any of them.

So, she helped me with the preparing and then after she left, I realized that I hardly had looked at her the entire time that she was here. I hardly had really looked at her ever in our friendship. I always was aware of her presence but not of her, herself. I finished folding the shirts we had mended. Samuel would be in at any moment. The dinner, simple as it was, was hardy enough.

As I folded the last piece, I used a hemmed corner of it to wipe some tears. The loneliness was of not knowing, hardly looking at this loyal friend, and it was - I could see how right she was - this loneliness was the source of wanting the gossip, wanting the ways I could talk in order to slur others just beneath the telling of events.

I put away his shirts and sat on the bed, the geese feathers in it never resisted me and they did not so that day, but I realized how some form of something pushing back at me, some basic clash with another, would fill the loneliness which then would make it worse.

I was sitting on the bed when Samuel and Mattias came in. I opened my arms and brought them to me with a big hug. How could I be lonely with these two mighty souls intertwined in mine? But I saw, as the hug disengaged, that this loneliness was on another level than the family love. There were two: one town built over another town that got forgotten. And the forgotten-about town was where somehow the gossip went and filled it with negatives about others. It was not a nice story down there at all, but at least there was activity where there had been emptiness.

At dinner, I used my large, rounded knife to cut through the chicken. How could a knife be so rounded - it also was wide this knife. I never got over feeling bad for my chickens since

I got to know them as I fed them over time and often watched them in my restful moments. But hunger pervaded and cut through that chicken in its round, sharp way.

Then Samuel would look over the account books and Mattias would play with Elbia, our cat. He'd be humming, my son, and we were seeing there was a musical ability in him that neither of us had. We would get him a fiddle as soon as those account books in Samuel's large hands would say we could.

That night in bed, I told Samuel all about this day's visit with Mrs. Whittaker and then with Matilda and what she said about gossip and security and how I realized I never really saw her.

She's been your guardian angel, he whispered as he fell asleep.

So, then I was awake thinking that over until the quiet of the night around me closed my inner eye and I slept.

Slept well I did and when I awoke, the two had gone to do the milking. I put the jam and bread out and had the grease melting on the frying pan. I gave Elbia some milk to stop her wailing purr.

We didn't speak much at breakfast as usual and yet, before he left, while he was getting his hat, Samuel said - men don't need to gossip that way.

Is that because you are doing the labor all day and no time for such? I asked. If you were in a room all day, would you then?

I could see that the question didn't interest him much, so I kissed him heartily and gave my son their midmorning food, hugging him so hard.

Yes, this silence that they left behind them, they do not have it daily. But there are the chores, I stay busy all day I thought as I carried the slop pails to the privy one by one.

Then the feeding the animals and starting to put together the ingredients for the lunch meal as I take down the clothes from upstairs to the washing. Most here wash only on Mondays, but I did it more.

I carried the wash boiler to the wash tub outside and scooped the hot water into it adding enough from the pump to make it warm and not burning. I prayed for Samuel and that he would have enough work this winter and get a good crop next year. I put the ashes and lye and the clothes in the tub. I prayed for Mattias, his health, and that he would find his music in this life. Then I rubbed the clothes on the wash-board and stopped to stir them with the dolly stick before I put them in the wash boiler and let them boil awhile until they went into the clothes basket to drain and then to my rinse tub. I prayed for our small community that it find and live in the eternal harmony.

It was so automatic and rhythmic all this motion, rather like as if I was spinning. So, that rhythm brought me to the for-gotten-about town beneath this town and there I felt for the human connecting. So, after I fed Samuel and Mattias at lunch, I took the wagon out and even let Elbia follow for a time.

The woods loomed large, and I recalled Mrs. Whittaker's parlor and I wondered if I ever would return there. I thought of the white tint gravel on her carriage drive. I thought how she lives in the upper town without even knowing she's lonely in the forgotten-about town and needs the gossip to fill her up. I thought of people richer and poorer than us and wondered about their relation to the loneliness of that for-gotten-about town. I took a penny out of my pocket and rubbed it.

In town I felt the bustle, I said my good afternoons and par-don me's, and with the penny I bought Mattias a peppermint stick. I went to see how much a fiddle would be. To fill my son was a kind of filling me, I saw that then.

Mr. Parker was old and especially kind to folk like me, it was as if he never had any inkling of the forgotten-about town and I thought maybe men in general didn't because they had women like his wife to give them that very warmth, the recognition-security of which Matilda spoke.

Indeed, his wife Mrs. Parker was a woman of a certain warmth, stability and kindness that was true. How did she deal with the forgotten-about town and her loneliness there when her husband went to his fiddle shop? I asked Mr. Parker if I could pay a visit to her.

Anytime my dear, anytime, in fact she is home now if you have a mind to go there. We don't need the calling cards, how we live, you know.

I may just go by, I said with a mixture of relief and tenderness.

No driveway there, no carriages, just a spot for the wagon to be by the house which was simple and all wooden. I pulled up beside it and felt more at home even before I entered. I knocked with an apologetic tone. I never liked dropping in on someone but there was no way to have told her before-hand. She was wiping her hands on her apron when she came to the Dutch door. She opened the top hatch first. Recognizing me immediately, she smiled and opened the bottom hatch to let me in.

She had been rolling out pie dough and I asked her if I could help. I told her I was sorry I had just stopped by like this and I relayed the conversation I had had with Mr. Parker. I told her that I didn't want to take time away from her chores and that I could just help her with them as we spoke. In no way did I want her to think that she had to entertain me.

I noticed some wool, knitted in a ribbing pattern on her side-board. A strange place for it, I thought. She bid me to sit and offered me tea. No bother, I said, I just wanted to visit neigh-borly and please do go on with your pie, that dough will right harden if you don't get back to it.

So, she did, and as she rolled it, I thought back to my wash-ing, my brooming, spinning and all the repeating actions we women do in a room. No wonder we find the forgotten-about town.

So, we spoke of our children and the weather and our crafts. I noticed she did not go to the gossip. What made it possible for her not to do so? Was she not caught at times in the forgotten-about town, and did she not want the mean thrill of talking about the others to fill it up there?

She lined the pie dish with the crust. She rubbed the baked apples through the sieve and mixed them with the powdered mace and cinnamon. She crossed thin bars of crust on top of the pie and put it in the cook stove.

Then we sat with tea. She spoke of her daughter's child; she spoke of her son-in-law and his work. Nothing was mean, nothing was of the gossip intending to hurt.

Do you have the feeling of security? I inquired gently.

What do you mean dear? She asked me kindly.

That you are recognized and not lonely.

Recognized in what way dear?

That someone sees who you are in the deepest part of why God made you and that gives you peace.

Like Christ seeing me?

Like that, but a person.

The Pastor?

Does he?
It's more my husband who does but it took a while and some challenge before he did.

I see.

Are you lonely my dear?

I am trying to see what makes all the gossip.

And you think that comes from the loneliness?

Yes, I do, like there's this empty, forgotten-about town beneath us and it's abandoned and some of us go to it and the loneliness is there and we gossip to not feel the meanness that can come from this loneliness, but then we become mean by the gossiping to not feel the meanness that comes from the loneliness. It's hard to explain.

I think I see it. I know the gossip. It is often between us women certainly. It is not considered a manly thing. They fight instead.

Do you know the forgotten-about town, so empty, so abandoned?

Yes, I do. But it's not just beneath us, it's all around us, and the men feel it too, but they deal with it by working and fighting mainly.

Fighting or gossip, I sighed, it's all meant to keep from the mean that grabs anyone in the loneliness of the forgotten-about town.

Dear, she said, getting up to check on the pie, yes, the mean-ness is there and comes from being in that town. We are a pioneer tribe, and the meanness is there, we abandoned our homes to come here, and we have been abandoned by those we love to come here and in this moving from our family from overseas, then from our family on the coast, there is the forgotten-about town following us, all around us.

You are smart like Matilda, I said.

Who is Matilda?

You know her I'm sure, she's from here.

No, I can't say I do.

She wise and a great helper of me. She guides me and tells me about the gossip and where it comes from.

She sounds grand. Dear, I just need to finish the ribbing on this scarf, would you like it? She went to the sideboard, got it and took it to me.

It's lovely, I can finish the ribbing and bring it back to you.

No, it's for you alone. It comes out of the forgotten-about town and it's not meanness.

So, there are gifts from there?

Yes, if you are patient and not afraid to stay in there for a while. But you have to get through the temptations of mean-ness to get to do what you can do that is of beauty.

What do I do if I get lost in there?

Call me or someone you know who is close to the Holy Spirit in the place.

Mrs. Parker, how would you hear me if you are not in prayer at the time?

Keep calling. And do you know anyone else who knows about the place? If not, call on the Holy Spirit - go right there.

Counselor.

Yes, Samantha, it's not just a song in Church or a Bible verse. It exists.

It or he or a she?

I think of it in my heart as she actually. The holy water that connects and gives life to all things. That's my secret in the forgotten-about town.

I could cry.

Sad dear?

Yes, for that I have this forgotten place be part of me, of my life, and then I get mad for my self-pitying.

It's not a bad place.

But it's a heavy thing. It weighs on one.

As womenfolk in the houses, we all go there, but not all of us recognize that we do, some think it's being moody or having the monthly, or a bad day or it's someone else's fault. The monthly and our relating to the oceans and the moon can bring us there but they are not a bad cause of it. You are fortunate, Samantha, that you can see where you are then.

It's all I can see then.

It's fortunate. And you still go be with the other women and those that don't know they go there who try to fill it with the gossip and the meanness. You don't need to tell them where they are, or they'll go after you like rifling a coyote in the woods - but you cannot take on the meanness as you realize that it's coming from their being in that town and not knowing the way through it or out of it.

But why can't they see the town and why do they choose meanness to fill it thinking they can get out?

I can't answer the first - that's something you only can bring to prayer. Meanness is a grating like we do with this cheese. And the touch and friction of it is filling enough for us to think we are getting out of that town. But it always comes back, it's around us this forgotten-about town, always.

And men aren't thrown in like we womenfolk because they're with one another concentrating on their outdoor work all day, right?

But they will be over the time.

What time?

When men and women both spend more time inside when the inventions take over, I can see it.

So, we women are like the first explorers of this forgotten-about town?

Yes, and Mrs. Parker laughed, we women are pioneers here and there.

She offered me pieces of pie to bring home to Samuel and Mattias, but I declined with a smile and told her that she had given me a hardy meal with dessert in her rich talk with me.

As I lightly swept the reins over my horse's side, turning the wagon around, I thought of Mrs. Whittaker's grand drive and her carriage and wished in my prayer heart that she too could speak with Mrs. Parker as I had done.

The ride home was much more peaceful than the ride out and I think my Bessie felt that peace of mine through her reins and through my hands because she went in that easy rhythm with hardly a look sideways or a whinny.

I gave her extra oats and rubbed her down with a prayer while seeing in my mind's eye my son singing his hymn. I placed my forehead and cheek against her neck, breathing in her heat and her strength which seemed part of the prayer, like the Spirit above knew this animal and they were often in a kind of speaking to one another. That kind of strength.

Then I went inside and finished making the dinner and sorting and brushing down the day so the menfolk could enter an unburdened house that welcomed their burdens, their tiredness, and knots.

There was no necessity, I saw, through dinner and afterwards, to tell Samuel about what Mrs. Parker and I had spoken. But I told him that it was a very good visit. He wrapped me in his arms, and we felt warm against one another. Here is another way to move through the forgotten-about town if one needed to, I thought, before drifting to sleep.

There was no way I could even consider the forgotten-about town during the next week with so many preparations for the Church Thanksgiving dinner. I had the duty of pies and our home became through and through with those sweet smells. It was a fun day for our small town, all were smiling during the feast which was the best meal most of us had the entire year. And we were smiling with the memory of what the day was in our bare bone history.

At one point, all the activity and talk were too much for me and my ears were wringing so I went out to spend some time with Bessie. My cheek was in its familiar place on her neck and my right arm straight across her torso hugging her when Mrs. Whittaker saw me as she was returning from the privy. I was surprised she had used it since it was not nearly as clean as hers, I was sure.

I thought how this gathering must be below her standard and probably was one of the poorer meals she had all year, but she looked calm most likely due to the whiskey punch that was plentiful. At least it was a day off for her kitchen maid and housemaid and I wondered what they were eating at this time.

She came over to me and asked me to come by soon, that she had the continuation of the story she had been telling me about the Smiths and the Tuckers. It was that mean gossip again finding itself all the way out here as I stood in my good heart to heart with my Bessie.

Then there was a glimmer in Bessie's eyes from the particular lowering of the sun at that moment, but I saw the flash and had an instance of a possibility: this was my test, this was the Holy Spirit coming to me to see how much I had learned from its giving me the forgotten-about town.

I told her that the day after the next two days would do fine for a visit, and it was then that I found myself once again walking down her gravel carriage drive.

She took me to the same chairs in the parlor in which we had sat a few weeks ago. But now I saw differently since I stayed in the forgotten-about town as she spoke. She was telling me what was wrong about the Church Thanksgiving gathering and what was wrong about Mrs. Fletcher's new dress and what was wrong about Mrs. Tucker's oldest child and wrong about Mrs. Anderson's spice cake and then she told me to sit up straighter in order to look more like a lady.

The line from my eye through heart to womb and back allowed me not to take in this negative or to reflect it back to her through sharp comments that were hidden in sweet tones. The line was throughout the secret town and connected all of us in it including Mrs. Whittaker though she did not know, was not at all aware that she was in it which was why she felt so alone and empty and was filling that with the thrill of negative talk that was little bits of dynamite attacking others to make her feel alive. Though it was through destruction it was still a connecting: brief, terrible and then gone back to a further emptiness.

So, as she continued with this speaking, I silently invited her into the forgotten-about town, to share being in it with me. We were sitting outside what was the deserted saloon in the deserted town. It was bleak, dusty and the surrounding hills were no solace, and, in this town, I took her hand, I let the pulse of my connection through the line to the town move on to her.

In the parlor, she offered me a piece of blackberry pie and then she began to cry. I had an old, embroidered handkerchief that my aunt had given me when I was fourteen. I handed it to her without getting too close and not wanting to embarrass her at all.

I remained silent and did not ask her anything. I knew from where those tears had come and it was good since they meant she was coming back to herself, her loneliness, acknowledging it firstly through her body.

I heard the housemaid in the hall, so I went to engage her in order to give Mrs. Whittaker some privacy. When I returned to the parlor, she was standing by the hearth, leaning on her left elbow. She was not speaking, which was so unusual for her, it made the moment rather uncanny.

I stood by her silently while I went back to the forgotten-about town where I was sitting by her on the steps of the saloon. A few people there passed us, walking to our right. They were shadowy and I didn't know them, but it was like I didn't have to know them. I looked at her as we sat there. Her bonnet was off, and her hair was down. She hunched over her knees. She lay her cheek on her knees looking at me. She said she was grateful.

By the hearth back in the parlor, she collected herself and called the housemaid. She requested two pieces of the black-berry pie. We ate it with black tea with a bit of cream. Her silverware was elegant and recently polished.

I spoke then about my family and the humorous and dear times at the Thanksgiving celebration as well as what I antic-ipated our Christmas would be like.

She nodded and avoided my gaze though her smile was sin-cere as I spoke. In the forgotten-about town, we stood up and followed the other folks and listened to their voices. As we walked, I noticed gravel with tints of white along the road. We weren't sure where we all were headed but we knew we were fine, and it was safe to follow them.

After the pie, as I was leaving, she took my hand. She said she would wash and return the handkerchief. She said that my visiting her had been a kind of relief, but she wasn't sure yet how. I replied: We can speak of it another time if you'd like. It's something I've been learning and just passing on. We're all in the same town.

As I walked back down her carriage drive, I picked up a few stones with the white tint in them. I heard: "Even the stones would speak." I put them in my pocket.

That was fourteen years ago when clock time met with Eternity in the way the forgotten-about town was given to me and through it I learned about people's disguised wording in meanness. Since then, I've gone in and out of that town which has allowed me to be a help to many including myself.

As I said in the beginning, you are a good attender so you may be thinking: Where is that town now? It is always around all of us. You may be asking: And what about those stones? They were and are with me to remind me of how Eternity intersects in a moment in our time and over time in timelessness.

You also may be asking: Where did those people in it lead you and Mrs. Whittaker that time? It was to an open field in which we gathered and through hymns and prayer witnessed the Spirit appear in various images to each of us specifically. Then we all called out "Mama" as we were so close to our most basic yearning. Since that Mama was long gone, we separated and went out to be alone to face our specific abandonments while knowing we were all together in Spirit in the forgotten-about town.

SARAH AND THE IDEA

A Young Adult Story

Sweet Girl

Sarah was a sweet girl. When I say sweet,
I do not mean cotton candy sweet.
Or cinnamon bun sweet. Or the fragrance
of a rose in a vase on the kitchen windowsill
that has been in the sun for a long time.
Or even the way we sometimes think that
someone has an extra kind way of speaking
to us.

When I say Sarah was a sweet girl, I mean
that she had an open heart and let others,
including me, see it. What is an open heart?
you may ask. It is not that anyone could see
her heart like they could see her eyes. But they
could see her heart through her eyes, and through
her face and hear it in her words.

Some people speak as if they have an open
heart, but their eyes and face show that they not
yet have been able to open their heart. Sarah

was different. She was able to open her
heart after she had many strange things
happen and this is how it all began.

She was born in a very poor family on the
'other side of the tracks.' That means that she
was not born in the part of the town where the
rich people lived with expansive homes and
expensive cars and lawns that looked like
someone cut each blade with a carefully
sharpened scissor.

She was born in the basement rooms that had
metal strips on the windows so burglars could
not break in during nights when most everyone
was sleeping. Most everyone slept except Mr.
Crimston who never could fall asleep at night
yet slept in the day. He was a retired man who
lived on the second story of their building. He
could spot the burglars in the night since he
was sharp sighted.

Sarah had a brother named Tom and a sister
named Fran. They were older and went to
school during the day. Sarah was seven going
on eight, and yet, because of a persistent cough,
she stayed at home with her mother who taught

her lessons. Her father worked in the train
station. He cleaned the trains and would come
home very tired with black marks all over him.

During the day, Sarah's mother would scrub
her father's shirts that had the black marks on
them. She would scrub them and then collect her
quarters, bundle up Sarah and they would walk
through the street to the Laundromat. It was very
cold out and the Laundromat was far away but it took
the coins and their clothes came out not completely
clean but clean enough.

Then they would go to the market and Sarah's
mother would get just enough vegetables and
bread for a good dinner. On special occasions, she
would get a bit of meat. The butcher thought that
Sarah's mother was a good person, though very
shy, and he sometimes would add a little meat
to her order.

In this basement apartment, Sarah slept in the
same tiny room as her sister, and Tom slept on a
rather tattered couch in the living room though it
actually also was the kitchen and the den. There
was a rug on its floor that had been left there and it
had a pattern of lines that, though faded, had

been colorful to the extreme at one time.

When her brother and sister were away at
school and her mother was busy cleaning and
sewing for other people, Sarah, while doing her
homework, would sit on the rug and explore how
the various threads were woven. She would follow
some with her eyes and some with her finger. She
would imagine what they looked like when
they first were made and when the rug
was strikingly beautiful.

Docia

And as Sarah would imagine the beginning of
the thread's movement to what would become
such a beautiful design, as she concentrated on
this movement, there was a little girl across the world
who was imagining how her toy, the one with the
strings, was made. She was Docia and she was
thinking of the skilled worker who had thread those
strings so carefully.

Docia lived in a poor village where her father
sold vegetables in the open-air market where
there was a loud mixture of shouts and noise
from all sorts of carts and wagons and men selling

their wares. The vegetables her father sold were very colorful and he would tell the people how healthy they were for them to live a long life.

Docia's mother was the woman who carried laundry from others' homes and did it in their own tiny home. The people whose laundry she carried had books on their walls in the same way that her home had plaster on the walls. Docia's mother would tell her daughter about the colors of these books and their names. She told her daughter that with God's grace there would be the opportunity for Docia to go to a school to learn to read.

By now you may be wondering whether Docia also had an open heart or if she was going to get one like Sarah would. Docia was also on the way to an open heart, and hers was not quite as closed as Sarah's. So, perhaps you ask, how did Sarah's heart close at such a young age? Are we not all born with open hearts?

That is a very deep and important question. When Sarah's mother would see her daughter look sad or lonely or closed down, she would tell her about hearts and how most were closed.

Sarah asked her mother why that was. Her
mother replied that each of us is born into a
certain family with certain problems and struggles
and challenges and those go right to our heart
from the minute we are born. Some of these
struggles close the heart right away and some
do so over time. But very few get to childhood
with a completely open heart. Yet, her mother
said, there are all sorts of ways that the heart
can open and revive out of these struggles.
This is a story of how that happened for two girls.

Sarah's Father

Docia was playing with her toy of strings and
Sarah was playing with the threads on the rug.
Then Sarah heard Mr. Crimston. He must be up
during the day today, Sarah's mother thought,
and that was unusual. He was moving his table
or something that sounded like that. Maybe he
was expecting a guest though that would be very
unusual. He was a quiet man who lived a quiet
life. He did watch over them though, he did
care about them and, if he suspected any
trouble, he would make sure that Sarah's
family was fine.

He had a grown daughter who lived far away.
She would visit Mr. Crimston every now and then,
mainly at holidays, but not too often. The strange
thing was, and Sarah felt such in her bones, that
Mr. Crimston never seemed lonely. He had his
drawing, his dog and his music. Even though
he was up most nights, his music never was loud
enough to bother them. In fact, nothing he ever
did bothered them.

You may wonder if Sarah's father and Mr. Crimston
were friendly. They were always polite when they
met and Sarah's father appreciated the way Mr.
Crimston looked over them as they slept, but they
never spent much time together particularly since
they slept at opposite sides of each day.

One day, a larger train came to town and two
older trains were sent to be scrapped. It was a
sad day for Sarah's father since he had worked
hard on getting those two trains clean and in a
way he got to know them like he would get to
know a friend. So when they were pulled out
of the yard, he felt little tears emerging from his
eyes. Others would think he had a cold since
he was not a man to emote much.

So now he had to get used to cleaning a new
train with new gadgets and seat additions and
modern appliances. It was indeed a most extra-
vagant train. It glistened. It spoke of the fascination
of foreign lands and languages that made one's
blood tingle. It seemed to be balancing on the
edge of great adventures. This is when Sarah's
father received the Idea. It came as a lightning
streak up his back up his neck and across his
forehead.

The Idea

With all his struggles, Sarah's father had been
clogged, parts of him had been shut down,
including his heart. It was because he had some
guilt and it was because he yearned for more
money for his family and he played cards and
lost money. It clogged him up since he never
told Sarah's mother and his yearning was turning
into a kind of secret greed that was closing
him up and hurting him.

So he woke up one day and heard Mr. Crimston
about to go to bed; he heard Mr. Crimston's
water glass that he kept on the side of his bed go
down on the side table and he heard Mr. Crimston's

dog jump upon the bed. He thought of the quiet
peace of that man and then Sarah's father
decided to go to confession.

With a smoothly quiet swish, the curtain of
the confessional opened, at first Sarah's father
only heard whispered words but then it all became
clearer and, as Sarah's father confessed his
greed and his envy of all those with big houses
and fancy cars and lawns that looked like every
blade of grass was cut by a carefully sharpened
scissor, as he confessed this greed, this envy,
the words burst out of him like the air that is
blowing up a spectacular balloon.

And the holy one seemed to be catching
this balloon and carefully letting out the air into
the sacred space where it merged with dust particles
and was changed to tiny sparks of light. Then
Sarah's father went home and was pleased to
find that the butcher, who thought that his wife
was kind yet shy, had given them an extra
piece of meat.

So now that he was clearer, less clogged
and things could move through him better,
this was when Sarah's father received the Idea

when he came on the sparkling new train. He sat
down on the slippery new seats that looked like
leather. He spread out his legs. He for once was
not worrying about the time or getting caught
resting. Once it came through him, he looked
at it. The Idea was so big that he had to
sit down to hold it.

When he got used to holding it, he turned it
around in his hands to see it at every angle.
To him, it looked good in every direction. It
was so smooth that even where it had angles
and creases, they were so small, like tiny shingles,
and so even they felt smooth. It was a very
smooth Idea.

The Idea Comes Home

Eventually as he held it, the Idea condensed
in size. As he held and looked at it, it became
more of human size. So Sarah's father went
into the bathroom and took some toilet paper
and wrapped it around the Idea. Then he
folded it and put it in his left back pocket.
It fit in there so tidily that it was as if there
was nothing in the pocket so he did not have
to worry about anyone taking it.

Then he got up, tightened his belt and went on
with his work. After he got home, he sat at the
small table in the room that was living room,
dining room, and kitchen (and Tom's bedroom)
and he went over what happened with his wife.
He took the toilet paper out of his pocket, unwrapped it, and the Idea bloomed like a
relieved flower out of its bud.

Sarah's mother looked at the Idea and gasped.
She had never seen an Idea like this so perfectly
formed and so evenly right. She turned it over in
her head and looked at it from every angle and
she smiled; it really was a great Idea.

Sarah was sitting in the corner, she was
playing with some strings she found in the
street yard two days ago. She was twisting and
swirling them around her fingers, making
them into a tent, a cart, a dog and then a
woman dancing. When her mother held the
Idea, it caught Sarah's eye and she looked up.

At first, she thought it was an animal like a
purring cat, but then she saw how pretty it was
and how light it was when her mother turned

it to look at it in every direction.

The door opened and Fran and Tom came
home from school. They were tired and hungry.
They may have been arguing about something
since Fran's face was red and Tom was un-
usually silent. They took off their shoes as
usual in the doorway. They were about to go
in separate directions when they saw the Idea
and they each, in their own unique way, lit up.

Fran reached out her arms to hold it. Yet her
mother put her finger to her lips as if to say:
Not yet, it is so new. Tom wanted to poke at it to
see if it was real. Is it real? He asked that about
three times. It is new and it is real, his father
replied. It came to me after I confessed when I
went into the new train for the first time. He
looked happy and so his children were
happy with him.

Fran was most curious about the Idea and
she scrutinized it. She had a fine eye for detail
and she was fascinated by all the curves and
layers in it though it looked so even and smooth.
She tried to look for messages within its fine
creases but there were no words that she

could see. That is what she hardly could understand: how could such a large, splendid Idea
have no words attached to it?

So, Fran asked her father, she asked her mother:
How could there be no words even in the deepest
crevices? Each of them came over, one on
either side of the Idea and they also looked it
over carefully. Their mother put on her glasses
to do so. Right, they each said, one after the other
(for they often did that), there are no words in the
Idea, none that we can see yet.

Well, piped in Tom, how do we know what it
is if there are no words? Their mother answered:
Just by looking at it slowly and carefully. Just
look Tom, she said, don't you see the Idea
and what it is? He stood there and looked
and then he nodded. Yes, I see what it is. It
gave me a tune which became a picture and
then I find the words. We all see it that way,
their father said, bending his head in a kind
of prayer. Then their mother suggested they
in fact pray for it, for being sent this Idea.

The family gathered in a small circle and bent
their heads and prayed in thankfulness. They

intuited that this Idea could bring a big change
to their family that was a positive change
though none of them knew how or why. So
they did sense it was a generous gift and
they were grateful, though unsure of why
they deserved it.

Ballerinas

Across the world, Docia put down the stringed
toy with which she had played. Her mother
came in with fruit and vegetables from the
market. There were hot peppers, lentils, papayas
and bananas, and she had been able to get
small slices of chicken as well since her
husband knew the chicken vendor and had
done him favors.

Docia's mother went to the clay oven and
began the preparation for dinner. The mud floor
was remarkably cool that day and Docia was
content to stay on it with her strings and watch
her mother at the oven that was generating
its small heat on the humid day.

Docia stretched out her legs and looked at her
toes which were wide across her feet. They

were not curved to a point like some ballerina's
but were almost straight across and rather pudgy.
But she imagined ballerina shoes on them
anyway. The shoes were pink, worn
from many hours of practice, satin,
torn in the right places.

She moved her legs as if she were dancing
and as if the strings on gallant utterly expensive
instruments were accompanying her with a
rhythm both serene and moving. She danced
in her corner for the entire time that her mother
prepared their simple dinner. That night,
after the three of them retired, she lay
on her mat, watched the stars and
saw the entire ballet, in her head,
in the stars.

Across the world, Sarah had a doll made
of old, worn-out cloths that once were her
family's clothes. She had knots for the
head and larger ones for the body and
slimmer ones for the legs and arms. She
imagined that her doll, who she called Janis,
was a ballerina. Sarah spent many hours in
the concert halls with Janis who amazed
audiences with her jumps, twirls, bows

and beckoning pirouettes.

Janis was the primer ballerina and Sarah had
other rag dolls who were in the troupe as well.
At times they would have arguments and even
fights among themselves. They would come to
Sarah to sort out these conflicts. She was good
at it. Her mother had taught her how to do it:
how to calm each side as she let each have their
say and then slowly start to speak to the other.

One fight was over a dress. Janis had two
ballerina companions who were in the dance
with her, as a kind of moving chorus dancing
behind her. The two argued over who should
wear which ballet skirt. The skirts were identical
but their colors differed: one was azure blue and
the other was turquoise. They were so angry
about both wanting the turquoise skirt that
they almost tore it in two until Janis came
to talk it out with them.

Sarah had Janis first listen to why each
wanted the turquoise skirt. It was for reasons
that were different than she would have thought.
One wanted to be the brightest on the stage, the
other wanted to look more like the water than

the sky. Then when each heard the other's
reason, they realized that they were scared
about performing and therefore were competing
with one another.

It was easy after that discussion to decide
who got which skirt since it did not matter
any more since the skirts did not hold the power
they formerly had. With her mother's help,
Sarah got better and better working out such
arguments between her toy ballerinas and also
she got better at putting on the ballet shows
which she showed to her mother.

This night, in bed for the night, Sarah whispered
to Janis about the Idea. She asked her doll:
Did you see it? Janis nodded yes. Did you
understand it? Janis nodded no. You just
have to look at it in a certain way, like this,
she showed her doll, craning her neck and
then the doll's neck. Do you understand it now?
Yes, Janis nodded. Then we will be very fine,
won't we? Janis nodded again and Sarah slept
very well that night.

Looking at the Idea

The next morning, all the family rose earlier
than usual and one by one they went into the
living room/den/kitchen/Tom's bedroom to see if
the Idea was still there. Their father was there first
and he was sitting on the floor looking up at it. It
had risen during the night so it was touching the
ceiling but it had not changed size or shape. It
was as if their father was trying to figure it out.

Their mother went over to him and put her hand
on his right shoulder. Her hand melted into his
shoulder since it brought him a graceful, quiet heat.
His neck felt weary from looking up ever since
he awoke, but now, with her hand there, his neck
was energized again, he could turn his head
without aching. So, Sarah's parents sat
on the floor for a time looking up.

Then Fran, Sarah, and Tom accompanied
them as each got up from bed. Tom was
yawning excessively but he trooped in there
after Sarah and Fran. The three sat around
their parents and also looked up. They were
hungry but it was like none could move, none
wanted to move. Suddenly Tom got his notebook

and rhythmically began drawing the Idea. He
looked up at it, studied it, and then he looked
down to draw it. The others wanted to look at
his drawing, but their heads stayed looking
up at the Idea.

It was Sarah who took the first glance at
his drawing. Her glance just lasted a few
seconds but it was complete and focused.
She felt a bit dizzy from swinging her head away
from the Idea to Tom's drawing and back again.
It is not what I see, she said very slowly and very
deliberately. Her parents immediately turned to
see Tom's drawing. Nor I, they said simultaneously.
What I see also is different, added Fran.

After she spoke, Fran got up to make them
breakfast. They all had a sense they were hungry
but had no sense how hungry they were. It
turned out that they were really hungry. Seeing
the Idea had brought up a certain and different
sort of hunger in each of them. It was the sort
of hunger that wanted to get on the beautiful
sleek chestnut horse and ride through the fields,
up and down hills never seen before or
even wished for.

It was the kind of hunger that was accompanied by a great love. This was the sort of love
that could not help but open and surround one's
pet of many years, the pet who saw into one's
eyes and knew one inside and out. It was the
kind of love between hot and cold, dry and wet,
mind and body, that made all such distinctions
fade away and know each other at last.

Sitting together at breakfast with this hunger,
this love, the family saw one another as if for the
first time. They instantly began to pray in gratitude
for the food and for one another. This was
something they often forgot to do, but not this
day or any day in the future. The mother closed
her eyes and they stayed closed afterwards
for she was in a deep, meditative grace. This is
when Sarah felt her heart opening.

After breakfast, Tom went into the bathroom
and came out and drew the Idea again. It
was slightly different than his first drawing.
He exhaled deeply and looked carefully at the
two drawings. The form of the Idea was basically
the same but the tone of it changed a bit, like
looking at red for a time one can see it more as
a bluish red. And then, looking longer, one can

see the whole thing tinged in pink, pink streaming
from it.

It softened him this tone, it made him feel
warmer inside and eager in fact to get on
with the day. He looked at Sarah and wondered what form she saw. That question mattered
to him at this time to a great degree. He was
about to ask but then his mother was rushing
Fran and him off to school. Don't be late,
she said, since the teacher will blame me if
you are late. On their way, walking down
the path that had azaleas on both sides, he
looked into his sister's gray-green eyes,
hazel would be too general a description
of them, gray-green, he decided, was
the best description.

Those gray-green eyes had seen him
through a lot. Bad things in many shapes
had attacked him over the years, not only
literal dogs but what could be like a wild dog in
many forms. Fran saw all that more than their
parents did. They now looked one another over.
Fran was like a paisley design. One never knew
which direction her colors would go but then
they always ended up in a design. It was best,

Tom learned early in his life, to stay moment
to moment with her.

Sarah Cries

When they got to school, Tom thought he
heard a sound from the direction of the roof,
but nothing was there, there was no sound.
In actuality, it was Sarah back at home, for she
had begun to cry. She was crying for the change
that the Idea brought into her home.

For even though her parents were calmer
now, this entry of such an unknown frightened
her. Finally, she let out her fears in her tears.
Her mother thought that Sarah had stumbled
on something and she went to pick her up.
No mamam, she said, I did not fall, but my
heart is opening and I cry because I'm scared
of what the Idea is bringing to us, it's so
mysterious, I do not like the change!

By now, Sarah was sobbing loudly and
wanting to kick her feet on the floor but, as
usual, and as all the people in that land were
accustomed to doing, she restrained herself.
Yet the tears could not be restrained, they poured

down the ledge that may have been a bridge
at one point yet now was the ledge of a vast
river system that poured over it making its
own waterfall. Hearts opening make
feelings come through that are true.

Her mother picked her up and carried her
closer to the Idea. By now, she realized that
all saw it differently. She wanted to ask Sarah
what she saw but also did not want to ask her.
Yet then Sarah volunteered: It's not what I see
there, mamam, it is just that it is different and
I never saw anything like it before.

Yes, it is just different, her mother replied,
but that difference is not going to hurt you or us.
We would know by now if it was since your father
and I spent much time with it, exploring it, praying
through it and for it and our relationship to it.
You can trust our sense my dear, we know
it is different but it will not cause harm. How
we go to it is the important thing: that will
make the difference in how it affects us.

Does that make sense to you, her mother
asked, what I'm saying? Indeed, Sarah
was comforted by her mother's arms and

the words that fell from her mother's mind
and heart to her mouth and then to her holding
arms. The words fell through her mother's
hold and the tears did eventually stop falling.
Sarah moved within her mother's arms for a time.

Then her mother began to do the ironing
for her clients. The sound of the iron
too was comforting, the sizzle, the guarantee
of smoothness and the regular, repetitive
swishing hiss. Her mother hummed as she
ironed and the tune synchronized with the
iron's sweep.

Then Sarah moved to their tiny mainly dirt
backyard. She noticed a butterfly chasing a bird,
or trying to chase a bird, from how it looked.
She got up and tried to follow them which
just scared them off and both were gone.
She sat back down in the tiny lawn, not really
a lawn since it had very little grass. It looked
like a bald man's head with just a few
strands of hair left.

You may have noticed that it was not that the
lawn looked like an infant's head with a few
strands just emerging. This is because the lawn

had a worn-out look, the kind of look that a man
who had been at a hard job for thirty years or
so might have.

The Moldy Tent and the Lavender Field

Sarah felt lonely sitting by herself on this
worn-out lawn. She huddled and held her knees
to her chest. Her mother was still singing as
she ironed and the sound of her voice carrying
through the tepid air was a comfort yet did
not quite cut into the loneliness which
covered Sarah like a moldy tent.

So, she sat in the loneliness above and
around her, the loneliness around which her
mother's song swam. I say "swam" because
indeed Sarah's loneliness was like sitting in a
moldy tent surrounded by water. Though she
could breathe in there, she was very much alone.
There was no butterfly, no birds, nothing but
the thick, stale air.

So, she concentrated on that - the air - and how
she was breathing it. Some breaths felt heavy
and that they hardly made it to her lungs and
some breaths felt smoky like they were

clouding her lungs but then some breaths,
the more she was noticing them, were lighter
and their smell was more like lavender.

So, Sarah imagined that she was in a
lavender field. This was a yellow-green field
filled with lavender blossoms. She saw herself
laying in this field and how she thought she had
to fight or compete with the others to get there.
But there were no friends there, there was no
competition. Just stillness and that lavender
scent signaling a soothing calmness.

Sarah! - her mother's voice broke through
the water surrounding the tent, broke through
the mold of the tent, broke through the stale air
in the tent and even reached her as she was
laying down in the lavender field. Sarah - Sarah - Sarah
the voice said three times. That was enough and
Sarah was now facing her mother, at the
ironing board.

Where did you go child? her mother asked.
What dream were you in? Sarah just looked at her
mother silently. Could her mother get to the
lavender field by just looking into her? Her
mother did put down the iron and looked into

her for a short time but had to attend to the
clothes once more.

So, Sarah realized that she could stay in the
lavender field and still be with her mother at
the ironing board. Somehow she had carried,
or something had carried, the lavender field
inside the house with her. Sarah looked up at
the Idea - still there perched just touching the ceiling.
Then she realized that it was because of the Idea
that she was able to go to and bring in the
lavender field.

Did Sarah's mother, who was a very careful
and attentive woman, know that the lavender
field had been brought inside? Not actually
since she had to get on with her sewing and
ironing since her clients expected it all done
and delivered by four o'clock. But later that day,
when they were eating lunch together, she
noticed that something was different with Sarah
who seemed older, more at peace and more alert
at the same time, and with a better sense
of humor. So in this way her mother sensed
the lavender field.

Sarah Goes to the New Train

The next day, Sarah's father had off from work
and he brought her to see the new train on
which he was working and in which he had
been given the Idea. As they approached it,
Sarah had to squint her eyes since the shine
of the train was so startling and seemed to go
around her not just in front of her. She saw
this light as it was surrounding her, and she felt
the warmth and then realized she was
in the lavender field again and
carrying it with her.

During the afternoon, the day before, when
she had helped her mother sort her work
and then accompanied her on her deliveries,
Sarah lost the lavender field. It just seemed like
it went away or that she misplaced it.
By the time she was eating dinner with her
family, she almost had forgotten about it as they
all spoke of their day. But now, approaching this
train, she again was in the field and she felt
the smooth wafts of its scented air fill her lungs,
pleasing, satisfying something deep in
her very inhalation.

Her father was opening the door to the train.
As with her mother the day before, the lavender
field did not seem to go to him or to affect him.
At least not yet, and Sarah wondered if her
parents ever would know it. But then she
was in the train and relishing in its glory and
splendor. She felt dirty in comparison and she
asked her father if she should have washed
before entering it.

No, he smiled and said looking at her. You
are fine, folks much dirtier than you will be
getting on and traveling on this train, do not worry.
And he lifted her in his arms and kissed her
on the cheek right by her ear that was listening
to him so carefully. Sarah put her head on
his shoulder before she looked around.
But then she saw the most marvelous things:
seats that had dots on them looking like
diamonds, carriers for overhead luggage that
looked like antique wooden cabinets made
by artisans from long ago, doors that lead to
further coaches which were both beckoning
and grandly lit.

But there was something else: sounds. Sounds
like little puppies playing joyfully, sounds like

the trees outside lending the train coaches their
roots for sustenance, sounds like children just
arriving at wonder within nature. Then Sarah
noticed, as she was looking around, that
the lavender field had come inside the train
and seemed like it belonged there.

Her father put her down. He took her hand
and they walked from coach to coach. She saw
the crimson velvet curtains on the windows,
and how they looked like the silky robes that
would cover the queens. Then her father sat
on a seat and placed her across from him.
He looked at her carefully. He said that he
and her mother had something to tell her
and they decided he would do so now.

She looked back at him in wonder. He
seemed changed - he seemed older as if his
hair was white though it still was brown. His eyes
looked sparkling as if the joy of the first warm
morning after winter lit them with hope. He said
to her: Never worry about the laws of the country
changing or wars or money or the lands or
getting less, you always will have this train
to come to and be safe.

I know father, she replied, because yesterday I
found a lavender field or it found me, and it seemed
to come out of the Idea that you brought home
from this train. Mamam seemed to sense it,
and now I will tell her about it too.

Sarah thought about how she also would tell
her mother about the moldy tent and her tears
leading to the lavender field. Her parents
would understand about being lonely and
sad in the moldy tent with the stale air all
hurting her lungs that was all under
water.

They would understand about her noticing
her breath which began to smell of lavender
They would tell her how being aware of her
loneliness and breath in the tent were a part
of getting to the lavender field, how they went
together and how the Idea brought it all to
her and would over her lifetime.

Her father was relieved when he heard about
the lavender field and that his daughter had this
place of peace as she lived in the world outside.
He reminded her that if that field ever slipped
away, she could find it in the train. Unlike the

old trains that were taken away, this one
always would be here. Sarah felt like she
wanted to cry and she was not sure why.
Then they went through a few more
coaches before returning to the family.

The Silvery Feather

On the other side of the world, Docia was
sharing a meal with her grandmother. Her
grandmother was showing her how to weave
and then they stopped to eat. As they sat on
the floor, knees almost touching, the yarns and
needles were surrounding them, mainly scattered,
though some were in their correct piles. Docia
told her grandmother that she wanted to be a
ballerina though she blushed as she said it
since she knew how outrageous an idea
it was.

By outrageous she meant that a small girl
living in such poverty could never take even one
dance class. Her grandmother took her hand,
she massaged it gently. Dreams are the very
fabric of life dear, she said to her, they are
more real in some ways than this yarn, this cloth.
Docia asked her grandmother: Do dreams make

the cloth? Does the fabric of dreams make
the fabric of the cloth?

It's not that way exactly, her grandmother
replied. But some dreams come from a holy place
and they are sent to us so we can know the designs
for us and understand better the designs on earth.
Her grandmother finished her meal and put down
her plate and began to braid Docia's hair and the
young girl finished her last piece
of flattened bread.

Docia's mother entered the small room and it
was clear that she had had a very hard day. She
hardly spoke to them at all and she went over
to the counter to begin cutting the vegetables.
In each slice, Docia thought she saw another of
her mother's tears. She wanted to go hug
her mother but then she heard her father's
voice in the yard.

Her father's voice was as large as the caverns
Docia imagined in the faraway mountains. She
wondered whether her father had room for her
mother in such a cavern of a voice. And was
it pretty in that cavern she wondered, were
there the long minerals looking like solid

shimmering icicles? Sometimes when her
father spoke, the words had some of that beauty.

Then she heard her mother crying as if those
very icicles had been cut down and were melting
mightily, flooding the cavern that had been
her father's voice.

Her father was speaking to her mother now
and the beauty of his voice did carry the flood
of this pain of his wife. Then Docia's mother and
father went outside and as she was left with her
grandmother, they looked at one another and
secretly prayed for what was transpiring
outside.

There Docia's mother opened up her pain
further to her husband. There was a circle of
loneliness in it that no one before had seen,
that she never had shown anyone, not even
her husband, not even the grandmother
inside. That day, that afternoon, Docia's
father got very close to seeing and feeling
that circle of loneliness. It was surrounded by
a metal that seemed to attract the negative
in people just to know it still was alive
and not just alone.

Docia's mother told her husband of all the
negativity that she had attracted that day.
In's and out's of negativity, people's knives
coming at her because they had no where
else to go and Docia's mother offered such
a metallic draw of them. Then Docia's mother
took a long silvery feather out of her pocket
and said: Here is one thing that touched
inside my circle of loneliness. You may
keep it as a memento. It's the closest
another can get to my circle without
harming.

Then they were eating dinner and her father
was quiet and her mother looked happier, her
grandmother spoke the most. Docia went back
to her dream of being a ballerina and how,
when the audience would applaud, she
would dedicate her performance to her
mother.

The Dance

And Sarah was dancing already in her
lavender field. It had the feeling of being
slightly touched by feathers but it was the petals
on the long stalks just barely meeting her skin,

in movement, and, at times, in rapture. Sarah's
heart opened even more with pleasure in this
dance. In the image, she wore a long delicate
skirt and she was happy with its length, the
way it gave her fluid motion without exposing
too much.

For the dance was her design, it was her
vocation. It was not that she was to be a
dancer literally, but that her life was to be
such a dance and she could only know the
movements of the dance by performing it.

That was what Sarah saw when she, alone
in the living room looked up at the Idea. Oh,
she realized, I am to be a dancer. It's a dance
only I can dance. I will be alone on the stage,
though at times others may join me. Without
rehearsals, they're just there in front of the
audience on stage with me and their dance
goes along with mine. But we don't know
that until we are all there.

And do you know who will write the dance
for you? It is her mother asking. Sarah has
been telling her mother about what she sees
when she looks at the Idea. Her mother says:

The Idea is a marriage of image and word in sound -
you looked at it and you saw the dance and you
heard your way to life. It is written beforehand -
but you are not a puppet, you get to have
a say.

I think I know how, Sarah said. How so?
Her mother was looking directly at her and
there was a glistening in her mother's eyes. I
can choose whether to do the dance or not.
Sarah's mother thought about her daughter's
response for a moment and smiled going back
to her duties in the kitchen.

Sarah saw a part of the banana skin fall to the
ground as her mother cooked. This could be the
place in my dance where it looks like I am
sliding, slipping, and falling, but I am not, it
is just the sliding part of the dance. I am
sliding into being 8, into being 10, then 12,
then 15.

Sarah and Mr. Crimston

Finally, it was quiet in the house. All were resting
after dinner, and Sarah heard Mr. Crimston
upstairs and that he was up. She asked her

parents if she could go up and visit him. They
agreed since it had been a while since Sarah
had done so and they knew that the elderly
man enjoyed Sarah's visits.

So, Sarah walked up the stairs to his
apartment. She knocked carefully on his
door. He would know it was her because
that was what they had decided: hers would
be the careful knock. He was sitting on his
rocker that was covered with the faded
quilt that a grandmother long dead had
made for him.

Mr. Crimston was reading the newspaper and
having his first cup of coffee of his day which
was most people's night. There was some music
playing in the background. Sarah liked it and
much later would learn that it was light
jazz.

He looked at her when she came in and asked
about her cough and told her that she looked
taller than when he had seen her before. He
also said that he saw her guardian angel right
behind her. This did not surprise Sarah because
Mr. Crimston often spoke like that, seeing

spirits and talking about God because he was
a religious man. Sarah knew that from when
she was very young, and he helped her
know God better.

So, Sarah asked Mr. Crimston what her
guardian angel looked like. He said:
She looks like a long stalk of lavender with beautiful
air around her smelling of it, calming and gentle.
Sarah asked him: Does she speak to you? She's
mainly looking out for you, he replied. Does she
know my brother and sister? And he replied:
They have their own, each of different
flower meadows.

Sarah smiled and went to sit on a three
legged stool near his chair. She looked over
at the newspaper on his lap and asked him if
there was any news. There won't be a war
today and not probably in the near future, not
here at least and that's very good news. Sarah
remembered hearing from her father that Mr.
Crimston hated war and thought it was not
a necessary part of humankind but was a shortcut.
She wasn't sure what he meant by shortcut
and never had asked him or her father.
She sat there and talked to him then of the

shortcuts people take in life. She realized how
she was learning to keep away from some
of them. Since her parents had to work so hard
for food and shelter, they could not watch their
children's every move so children had a lot
more freedom than in other times
and places.

And there had been that difficulty: once Sarah
and her brother were walking home and they
took a shortcut and they saw a little dog hit
by a vehicle and Sarah was stunned for days.
Tom had run for help, but it was too late for the dog.
Sarah kept away from that area, the place of
her terror and sadness, for all this time.
She didn't want to make Tom sad or afraid
so she stayed away from the place and
tried not to think about the incident.

Sadness does not have to become an illness,
Mr. Crimston told her at that time. It can just
be sadness and then we can move on, to other
roads. But shouldn't we try to forget it? Sarah
asked. No, we don't try to forget. If we try
to forget too fast than the sadness doesn't
leave on its own and we can become ill. Maybe
now you are letting in the sadness and talking

to me so your cough can go - your cough
both was calling for the dog and not
wanting to return there.

He told Sarah that maybe she had taken
the shortcut away from feeling so sad about
the dog and all the fear of being there. But
that shortcut was clogging her up and making
her cough. So, he added, we learn to figure
out which shortcuts are not good and which
are good.

Some shortcuts can be good and open our
hearts more, Mr. Crimston told Sarah, but others
we do for ourselves only, to protect ourselves
or to get things in life in a cheap or fast way
that is not right for others or ourselves. There
are different shortcuts. Then Sarah decided
to tell him about the Idea since her family did
not keep much from him. She knew the Idea
would be a secret for those not close to them
but not for Mr. Crimston who was like part of
the family and protected them.

He sat for a while after hearing about the Idea
and he was scratching his chin. He finally said:
Just hearing about it, I am compelled to pick

up the newspaper and find something for you.
What does compelled mean? Sarah asked.
It means that I'm urged or encouraged to do
it by the Spirit. Sarah looked on as he picked
up the newspaper and went to a particular
page and searched through it.

So just telling Mr. Crimston about the Idea
passed the Idea on to him and it was that Sarah
was to have a pen pal. First, when he heard
about the Idea, he saw a young girl chatting
with Sarah and then he thought pen pal. This
page in the newspaper had a list of possible
pen pals. He told Sarah to find a name
that she liked, that appealed to her.

Her new pen pal was named Docia. Sarah
was happy with the Idea which is what Mr.
Crimston saw and heard as he looked at what
her father had carried home that day from the
sparkling train. Mr. Crimston told Sarah that
he also would help her with her reading and
writing so she could write to Docia.

So, Sarah and Docia began to write to one
another. They began to write a story of
ballerinas. In this story, the ballerinas were

dancers who did not compete and whose hearts were open. Docia and Sarah, though from such different parts of the world and having such different lives, related in ways that would last and be the foundation for future loves and many relationships.

MAE

A Prose Poem

The girl was wrapped in the cloak
she had chosen and is sitting left
beneath the thistle bush that at times
would bloom yet not today. To her right
a fruit tree emanates gems luscious
from the sap of branches long wearied
from elemental plights. Luscious fruits
too much on the edge of bursting to be
found in word or adjective, beyond both,
living in the image yet contesting neither
semantic nor word.

The sky overhead no longer broods
yet hardly perceptible the edge of
its smile. Come to the fields girl and
lay with me and the eager grass will
protect us. Who says it or why it is
said is not in her grasp and, in fact,
she hardly hears it at all. Come to the
fields girl, again it is said. Not thwarted,
she stays huddled. The only thing that
stays her attention is the low throated

pitch of which wild bird above, straight
above and veering east. Stays or got
or deserved her attention.

She touches the cross which is in her
heart, the very one once accused of being
black. Yet the bones of those not-of-blood
ancestors are dry white ash and their
spirits smile as their toxins alchemize,
transmuting and her efforts not unsung
were cleansed, the cross is indelible and
it remains, it is not weary as are those
branches of the fruit tree to the right.
The cross had long been beyond the
fruit. Capsules of understanding.

The string on her neck had wanted
pearl when she was younger, and she
had clutched to the want. The narcissists
had come and gone, she was left with wet
streams and her cheeks got accustomed,
her veins there cracked. The string is a
single woven ring with thread of a diameter
millimeter. It's relation to cross is her
hand touching them each in a succession
without purpose. Where will ring of neck
and cross in heart take the hand next

and which leads, here the unknown,
the yet unsung.

The grass beneath the thicket of thistle
was not expecting her, but it did adapt
and did not succumb to repellent. She
was not aware of hiding but more resting.
The days became longer. The cat she
had cherished was long gone and the
way her hand gravitated more to cross
in heart was with now a fluidity. She did
not trespass on her way there any longer.

Her palm to cross and the little buds
appeared in it. The tendency to call
such tattoo, the ways she had averted,
she had postponed. The carrier pigeon
called again up high. She looked up
but so swiftly it was like she had not.
Hand to cross hearted and the words I
will love you no matter what engaged her.
So, the simple threads around her neck
no longer caught.

As far as the cloak, it hid her since it was
invisible. The thicket groaned: Does not
anyone see who I have beneath me?

Even the cherished cat was gone. And
the busybody no longer or even kept
watch. The details of those conversations
were on what external distract contour
and, though she had participated, her
sense retracted from it all. Left in the
dust, that also, the daily conversations
of the glitter of hours leaving one hungry
and retching with hands outstretched
and fingers spread.

Crouching beneath the thistle thicket, she
remembered the trays, and vehicles and
the supposed rides on the top of what long
ago would be called trolley. Then she
smelled it first, the discharge from that
tree of gem, the illuminated fruit, from
its bottom out the roots to the ground
that did receive it thickly voluptuous
and viscous.

The discharge had its own intent unknown
to her. She was tempted to see it aiming
for her yet recognized hubris. The discharge
slowly and almost with a care ignited and
the gentle flame then licked the ground of
its ruined carcass remnant. When does the

purification overcome all that would be life?
Her eyebrows were on the edge of being
singed, and just as suddenly all fear
left. Her breathing reminded her of a
lullaby never heard but possible always
there in air, palpably ready to manifest.
Her breathing was not the lullaby but
it recalled it to her.

The time passed without any urge from
her to stop it or remove herself from it.
No clutch and instead a steady move to
the right-side pocket inside invisible cloak
in the almost-silk lining. The little book
in the almost-silk lining was Little Women
rewritten so it did not need so many
pages. She leafs through it. The main
message carries itself across the threshold
for it had been over her heart pocketed
too long and now belonged side pocket.
Leafing through and do not ruin the
ending. The sister had said do not
ruin the ending but I know that
Beth dies.

She turns her head for the first time to
look upon the discharge and there is

growing out of that ground now slivers
of grass. Sliver blades so young though
do not choke as the wind touches and
moves through them. Little Women: no
cat thrash nail gore or even the unspoken
intent, yet Beth dies, sacrificial love and
the other sister gets him, so remaining
little, women. Writing a story of compensation
or truth. She prefers truth which is being
beneath the thicket near the gem tree
discharging.

She sighs and takes a rest later called
long. A sound outside thicket so she
opens ear to the tree that has become
revitalized by the discharge and is saying:
To my right. And there the paw and there
the snort. Not the bear of berserk since
that novel was written. But bear out
and whisper and gag until the tepid off-
white stone with the silvery specks
emerges wholesome and as if almost
just bought. Stone that stomach repels,
this bearing can swallow only so much.
And it was supposed to be another sort
of gift. This bear, forestalling the nails
being painted orange-red, the color of

the season, the bear plods to the very
thicket and plops the stone by her side
beside and she thought she saw the
tree nod in favor.

Going to its reach, to reach for it and
she smiles and swallows the tears
finally done shedding for the doctors
gone wrong, who could not diagnose
on time and in the proper measure.
She swallows and the hum now from
above, call it urrr sound, call it uhmm,
it hums but does not negate the
possibility of machinery in it. Within
a smile, she swallows saliva yet the
tears remain drying and her cheeks
no longer sense soil.

The adventure of this hum so she looks
up through the bramble without any thorn
necessary to go into eye peer, enough
within her skin. She looks up and the
banner, for that is what it is, is yellow
pale yet its own fit of announcement
saying Hurrah Sarah. Sarah, pregnant
or not, Sarai, not pregnant and where
the wait, where the envy, what is in

whose design. Can envy be a way to
prevent birth, what is wanted to live?
The rest is history.

The line occurred Abraham Isaac Jacob
Joseph though Ruth and Boaz and the
next Joseph the silence understandable
how the Teresa could seize him and
squeeze him and the delight became
convents and that awesome seven
mansions and Bernini did not know
her delight after all though he thought
perhaps he was imitating it, it was not
directly from angel lance or even as
Lorca thought from duende or Lacan's
imposition yet from a holy profusion
through the most silent Foster Father
of the line's long culminating charge.
Inheriting it directly.

When the bear retreats she claps
repeat and rise to the banner becoming
balloon yellow still tinge says look to
what now more semblance of joy,
what are the letters on it, she squints.
The tear from her eye's corner since
the balloon brightens sky without

intent, without meaning to do so. Yet
it happens and the wide berth of light
pulsates, she thinks it also may have
been from her clapping. The billowing
forestalling letter and at first it is a
great relief, yet then the tongue silently
forms word almost it is a craving.

The quenching as speak. She
mentions a name, and then another,
a third and the sparkles from what could
be the illumination banner then balloon
manifest as this sweet sentence. One
sentence aloud. She looks around.
She wraps her legs closely to her and
her leather shoes look too young in
style for her. Bobby socks ribbed and
frayed now enough to finally in their
last gasp be removed, let some squirrel
nest in them.

Shoes stay removed, she now is a
lady yet thicket says, a lady dismissed,
not properly enchanting thus ignored.
But the bare feet get close to the
ground that which holds fast and holds
together, so many waterways and even

lairs beneath and this ground holds.
Her feet welcome and thank it
simultaneously. Her feet are soft and
extremely pliable, they want nothing,
they are almost flush, the flush of this
new encounter with natural solidity.
She sighs as she begins to stand and
the thicket roof prickles her neck,
head bent, this thicket allows not a full
stand. How to move without the panic
bears upon her though that one is
long gone.

And then the frame presents itself.
She is not going into a space of
amplitude so huge to be terror. The
frame of her vision sustains her. To
only be where it is that she sees.
The frame is not actual gold yet ornate
enough and so not blinders. The word
she was about to speak runs out of fuel.
She never knew who or what supplied
the first trickle of it. She recalls the
thirst and the quenching with that
first sweet sentence.

She huddles again thinking and so

the implosion was bound to occur.
Compression on a chest and something
turning a screw into very chest and the
pressure created around that exponentially
flows into the compression so she literally
moves over so she no longer is in the
same spot. Call it pressure, call it
implosion, they are only words and
either have or have not anything to do
with the intent of the very screw the
aim is direct not right to the heart but
mid-chest right beside it. To turn
nonsensibly is not enough, what
the intent.

It is when she is not looking out of
thicket, not at what was bear then
banner now balloon now wisps of air
wave for swallow, not looking out and
bent within it and the screw turns mid-
chest align to its contorted gasping
strolling twirl. Screw turns and here
the momentum larger than the very
twirl for her to get out. So that the
intent. Yet there are no thicket
cutters here. Screw motion says move.

She places her palm beneath the
lowest rim of thicket and asks if
rooted to the ground in the negative
she lifts it, ever an inch and then
further. Not alarmed. She passes
her hand through it and meets air
that seems open mouthed. Simple
curious reach yet with a bracelet
now of slivers of red where thorns
hold on, whispering do not go, do
not leave. Nails to dig and yet this
minuscule tunnel is not useful. But
the screw has had its time and twirl
abates.

She sits and waits and once again
looks out. The sky has grayed; the
crows replace swallow. The edge of
a purple cloud yet there is no yellow
here, no word, no communication
whatsoever except stay. She looks
upon the thicket in this manifestation
of her own being's neglect as well as
its retaliation supposed protection.
She touches a thorn at the roof of the
thicket, close to her head. Just a soft
movement. Along the side of thorn

she courteously avoids prick which
actually exaggerates tip. Then another,
stroking its side and avoiding tip pricking.

Her blood bracelet has closed into
new flesh so it no longer draws eye
or even can be seen. She closes her
eyes and tries to stroke another thorn
without touching tip. She senses that
she has to approach tips ever so
carefully. Yet none of it opens thicket,
it still bears upon her. Once considered
her home, once considered safe, secure.

All there is to do is to return to try to find
her body. Breathing deepens and pours.
She removes the political maneuvers
from her skin. The hurt is bearable. They
are dry skin almost scabs from times of
education throughout centuries. Now she
tries to stand in the thicket and she can
stand full height. There is a bird just
outside it and it is not crow, it is not
sparrow. Divided attention, hear it as
herald return to this skin find it. She bends
to the grass beneath her and rubs its oils
up and down her and they become

angelic gift. Now she stands and her
head does not bump into the thicket roof.

When the dimensions of what she is
under become manifest, when she
becomes aware of where she resides
under reaches. To the side of a house
and directly at a basement window. All
this time, she realizes, the thicket bush
has been on the side of a house,
perhaps a home. Some wilderness
fantasy subsides. She lowers to the
pane yet tapping does not resolve
what questions. She tries to figure a
way to open this pane yet wonders why.

This touch, tapping and the cool pane
does not recede. Tapping and then
soft rub along it and her finger has
smudge. Short, slight movements of
only forefinger as if there is a special
language to get through. She pauses
to her intent to get through pane means
to reassemble in someone's lived world
the basement of such. The thicket all
this time has been a hedge, maybe
a decoration of someone's lived world.

To go beneath thicket is not possible nor
is leaving it by going into basement of
another's life. To sit and look at this
smudge upon forefinger is possible.
Ashes ashes we all fall down, medieval
chant to forestall plague but there is
no plague here.

Come child do not cry, the old chant
too well worn and she swishes it with
her hand's slight sure motion. And no get
up and read either yet the restless heart
is true until and she touches again her
cross. Resting, restful now. Apparitions
they call what visions not yet acquired.
She waits. There is a song and there
is no bird now. There is a chant and
it is not of the child or for the children.
Little Women went away a while ago
as did the cat as did the bear, but
she still has the white stone with
silver specks and she looks at
that now.

Take the time sunshine, here is another
voice, more mature yet not deceptively
alluring. Virtuously alluring they once said

of the sensuality that is divine. White stone
with silver specks becomes the one in the
vision, the one carrying the sorrow of all
her children with a love unexplainable,
could never not be sensual, that look
that does not pierce or penetrate yet
knowingly concedes as informs is
sensually alluring as virtuous. Purcell
worked that out a while ago. He was
someone perhaps in a dream or old
memory and perhaps she sees him now,
finally, happily married with one child and
one on the way.

The question of what to eat beneath
thicket never emerged as question
since there was enough supplied perhaps
by the hands of Eros' mansion when
Psyche was fed, bathed, and sung to.
Perhaps those or the hands of the
Handless Maiden. But there was food
delivered enough. Not scrumptious
or plentiful yet enough. She remembered
St. Catherine in the cell for years by the
side of her parents' home imitated by
Jeanne of Shadows on the Rock but for
many more years. Imitated by other soft

souls with that requirement. But that
it was thicket this cell she never
questioned or even had the thought.

The extroversions went their way as
well as the vistas once necessary. So
now she looks out and there is nothing
there seen before and not exactly a
desert either. There is the soft gray
landscape with softer streaks of mauve
and tan and a sky that is very courteous
in touching it. She breathes into this
land and it seems as if it may open at
times to sprout or bud but that is the old
dream and she knows it. Take the time
when such is landscape, such is thicket
home and shelter. For that it was, and
somehow when the landscape moved
to rain or snow, she was protected. The
thorns would not fall onto her, the thorn
in her skin forestalled such. The thorns
would not bend to enter her in any way
or from any degree of might, manipulation
covert or other.

Prayers come with no hesitation or
hiatus, nor rushed nor compulsively

protracted. Nourishing and then there was one flower dropping in when unknown how. It was fragile enough yet still whole and it was a sweet magenta not overbearing or even bright yet soothing visually and through fragrance. Her eyes which had begun hurting no longer do just at the look of it.

She is hesitant to touch it as if it was an ice blue egg still warm from the nest when any touch would repel mother. Her heart that had been becoming parched takes the time and it is three in the afternoon and she sighs with the larger under-standing of how sacrifice engenders such a gift to one in need not knowing the need, this bloom. From St. Therese or Mary herself warming that daughter inside her that springs a warmth long solidified and immovable as inviolable even as if in a harsh demanding winter.

It still is the wide expansive vista with no flower there but here this one,

keeping company. Communion of
saints reminding. She slides down
and looks into it, into its cracks to see
if there might be the dirt encasing
if there might be that worm. In the
search, she falls asleep. She is
guarding a post in the dream, it had
been the source of violence with the
heads on the fence pickets and the
Kurtz like foaming within the hut.
She goes closer to the hut now and
the one with her, of that land and
decorated in its painted designs
all over limb and chest, that one
warns her but does not go forward
with her.

And, in the dream, his company is a
sort of a permission or even drive
to go further. She sneaks up to the
window and waits to hear what is inside.
The man there is grumbling, and he is
almost not a man, he has been once
virtuous and using his brilliance wisely
but now he has succumbed to the
addictive comfort of greed. He got
too lonely and the tribal queen never

really understood him or he her; he
used her to his own purposes and
though she adored him it was not the
love of companions of the heart nor
of the Intended that and his loneliness
became his ruler and he succumbed
to the ivory that could be seen, could
be touched and could hint at a final
unequivocal reward.

He rumbles around there and a
chair falls over. She gets scared and
runs and her companion speaks
something in his broken dialect but
she cannot understand it and wakes
up. Then she prays and she
inquires this man-monster who has
been in the hut who is before her
and so within the bloom of Mary's
mantle she inquires him. He is mute
and he only looks at her from the
most recent corner of his eye yet
he is not violent now. He is wanting
to go on in his nap resisting the child
who needs him to do an errand
involving travel.

He is sneaking into the bathroom to
have a cigarette when he said he
had given them up. He is typing
upstairs while those he thinks he
loves are attacking themselves and
one another downstairs. He is
threatening to kill himself if the woman
does not serve him, and these threats
are more insidious when implicit. He is
making sure his every desire is met or
that he can meet it while others look on
impoverished. He is always hungry and
completely incapable of knowing how
to get nourishment and possessing
feminine beauty has become the
only solace.

She inquires him and the threads are
veins through the flower petal tickling
or scratching they keep her alert which
keeps her modified. And the worry
comes up, just being with him, the
worry and the rumination and the fear
of being once and forever slashed. She
can hardly be in his vicinity without this
dis-embarking, this unraveling happening
in her brain sinew and skin.

Here is the screw in the chest, that
history and the formidable pressure,
it becomes clearer now the source of
such which sears to changed. To know
this man-monster is to not be propelled
so much through pain, and to be part of his
transmute is the discovery assisting new
generation. Those papers had been
written and she has practiced the
alchemy well. Now she sits and
looks at him.

A bellowing sorrow is in her chest
becoming the deer and three fawns in
the woods meeting highway at the edge
of the highway dangerously close with
the cars whizzing by so close, so
dangerously close. That sorrow, that
sorrow that seeps and is laden with a
memory now wisdom and she recognizes
it is Mary's this sorrow for the children
for the human race but she has it
now facing this man-monster of which
it had been amply written and revised
for seemingly eons.

And he is looking at her now. It is not
the same as St. Anthony's demons
or those of Fr. Pio. For he had come
to who is of another gender. The cry
from her chest now is more direct and
sudden and is on its way of leaving.
He is sitting with her in the cell of
thicket as it would be. The flower
that came in is also around.

There is the subtle sound of a flute
and the sound carries all the losses,
those seemingly trivial at the time and
those mightily devastating, those not
all her own, many of others not having
been registered or felt or examined or
relieved. She sits and faces him and
the eye doctor who had been idol gets
up from the desk in front of the line
waiting for him and finally is speaking
on the phone in another language. At
first, she thinks it is Italian, yet it is
another one, more New European.

The man-monster has been so many
and it would be too easy to bring
Christ to him or him to Christ. Christ

is here and is why the man-monster
can be here. It is not an intentional
thing. The fire that Bertha began was
not a will from the Rivers' household,
though getting the money willed was
contrived. So, she sings a song to him
and the flute stops, it is archipelago.
It is a ballad and in alto and he seems
to understand if not the words then
the melody. What transpires will. She
waits and sings, more softly now but
it is not to lull him there is no intent,
just sing.

He moves his left arm just a bit and
there is hair on it that had not been
washed for a time. She moves her
hand to it and he does not attack
or withdraw it by startling. She
touches it. It is granular and the
hairs are oily like the skin of Turkish
oil wrestlers. He could pin her down
in a moment but she knows this oil
wanting no longer the brute force
of another's man's muscle. She puts
her forefinger between the hair on
this granular skin and thinks how even

granular ice is slippery and can lead
to a fall so she is careful. She moves
across it collecting the oil of other
hair as she goes and easing it into
the skin. Now she is to the elbow. He
is making a sound, it is in another
language. She thought it was Italian
but it is not. He had been the one
whose mother had wanted to be
another gender.

She eases towards him. She puts
her ear to his ear and he is still. She
hears him for the first time, out of his
ear the meaning comes. They have
a discourse this way, ear to ear. The
hair on his head is not oily and so, she
notices now, his hair on his arms, are no
longer oily. The sport will be that of
another land. She combines the
ingredients. She gives him the proper
nourishment. He stands up and the
thicket allows it. Then he is gone and
she is walking outside the thicket,
without blood stains, without mutilation
of any sort or shape.

The air is strange yet vital. She lets
it in pore. She is not at the point of
rejoicing. The strength it takes, well
that is in her body's hair now and her
limbs are ready. She pushes against
what says stop, retreat. She thinks of
all the caves: Elijah, Lazarus, Benedict,
Anthony and Mohammed. She has not
time to wonder if she will miss the scent
of the thicket's must. She pushes on
and then she opens her eyes. The
blue has so much white and sheen
in it that it is startling. She sees
cities within it but she is not going
to a city after all.

The ground is supple and does not
react. Then she sits, the steps can
only take her so far after the entrance
to this air and the leaving of the thicket.
She sits or else she would dance. There
is no one here except the daughter so
she looks out with compassion. The
even breaths are almost impossible.
So, she stops completely and realigns
to focus on breath and to even them.
Then she knows her shoulders still

are carrying the burden of the leaving.
She lowers them closer to heart and
torso and thereby emits a sigh. It
is not loud at first but then the next
one is louder. This is not the exact
same moment of grace of one who
is tubercular and perhaps finally
resisting the abusive world. But
that is in her mind also.

Breathing evenly now and her
shoulders are softer. The daughter
is in front of her. The shift she is
wearing is light enough and Mae
stands and continues walking in
this new vein.

THE NIGHT WALK AND THE WATER

Remember Mama when the time had come and it was all gone and I put out my hands, palms up: all gone. The curious tone surprised us both. But my mother was not there, no longer there and that is how it had to be. He shook out the rest of his laundry and folded it. He always had been very neat. His shoes needed polishing, but he was neat, not meticulous, and he put them on anyway.

He sorted through the old addresses, as if he had the old-fashioned rolodex in his mind and figured out who he had to contact that day. His boy was playing in the sand outside. My boy is not as neat as I am or was at his age, he thought. He picked out an orange on his way out and sat down by the boy and shared the fruit with him.

Dirty smudgy hands and the juice of an orange making gestures as my boy describes the imaginary dump trucks doing wondrous things in the sand. It was not a sandbox exactly yet a patch of sand that I had left intact for his play. I also had envisioned friends of my boy playing alongside but that sadly was not coming to be: he had said that he had friends at school yet none ever appeared at home nor were there many party invitations. But my boy seems content enough in his introversion and I'm not oriented to diagnoses, in fact, rather allergic to them.

Marty, I said softly, what would you like for dinner tonight? Hotdogs and kraut came out as the expected reply. Then he saw the cut on the boy's hand between the forefinger and middle finger. It had begun to bleed some. Was it a rock? I asked him, how did you cut your hand? Marty shrugged, not invested in anything bordering on tragedy, which was a welcomed response, I always had thought, in a child.

As he returned to the house for a band aid, feeling dissociated from himself as usual, he wondered about the boy's blood. Where was his mother's contribution to its makeup? Once he had asked directly to her face: *Who* are you? That had been in the height of turmoil when he was incredulous about her behavior. Marty hardly asked about her anymore, but I knew he wondered almost unceasingly if not unconsciously about her.

I cleaned off and bandaged his hand and got ready for work. I spoke with him on the way to school about what he thought they would do in school that day and also about the benefits of a dinner healthier than hotdogs. He seemed quieter than usual on the ride in.

Hello, Joseph, hi, Joseph, good morning, Joseph - here were the echoes of salutations as I walked into work and I knew I should be grateful for such since there were so many such environments where even such a small gesture of kindness was not forthcoming. The days I cried when she left and had traces of crying when I entered this building, well, then they greeted me more earnestly yet even when said robotically, at least it was said: Good morning, Joseph.

I'm going to pass this ball of knots to you, Scott said as he gave me the files. He looked eager, his cheeks were pinkish, and he even emanated a robustness somewhat unusual for him. What's going on? I asked him. The guy next door is selling out and we may acquire the building to expand. Do we have the capital? We'll find it.

And Eleanor's pregnant she thinks, we're walking on air! Vast expansions! I exclaimed clapping my hand against his shoulder as his grin expanded as well.

The grass under him doesn't grow much, I thought, he is a mover. And I thought instantly of my own stalemates. The sourness of my dwelling in loss and the son who had to witness if not carry such. But I will not be dimmed today by remnants. Moves happen. Movers and shakers. And to do such without denial of all that went before... No denial but no quicksand either. He realized that he had been looking at himself from the outside again. But he had learned that the interior life was not a chore.

He lit the last cigarette of the afternoon and returned to his office, further untying the knots in the files that Scott had handed him. Then it was sundown, and all the lingering and sticky memories finally began to let go as he walked into that post-sundown night as his son slept. What dreams his son was having that accompanied and perhaps even moved his father forward in that walk were not explicit yet felt. He felt energized, motivated, even inspired to walk into the night.

Step after step I walked. It was not a staircase or even an incline. It offered no resistance yet the very darkness itself was inhibiting. My son slept calmly. I did feel his dreams come upon me. Do not give up, father, they seemed to say to me.

Give up to what and for what? He wondered. He picked up a long stick along the way that appeared almost as whittled to his purpose for leaning when the terrain got tiring and also for pushing aside any interceding brush.

Swoosh but gently do not break branches or damage the leaves, he thought: they are not in my way on purpose. I hardly look ahead on the path; it is too dark to see much anyway, so my focus is on each step. Then the darkness seems to move around me as if a small wind swirls clockwise with me as a center, my arms stretch out now to feel this change, like the hands on the imaginary clock. I am breathing less regularly.

He noticed that the swirl of darkness did not impede his steps or alter his direction. It was around 2 am in this moving forth after sunset, not 2 am on his watch yet in this post-sundown-night that he walked into and through. Then he thought he heard his son stir. He almost stopped. It all seemed so senseless at that point, why the move into darkness at all? He stumbled. There was a thin layer of moss over some of the stone on his path. He decided to lay down for a time. His chest felt very heavy. But it was his son who stirred in sleep who urged him to get up and continue. So, I did.

As I resumed this journey, I remembered the way she would dye the top of her hair magenta. Some children at his son's school would be in awe of her and others would be afraid of her. I had thought that the memories had successfully disengaged but for some reason this one still clung. It had no impact on my resuming this walk but I didn't want it, I didn't want even the image of this hair of that woman any longer. It can become a haunting, I knew that, and that I was on the edge of such.

And then I saw the rest of her body and she was beckoning me. Is this the darkness I walk within and through? Is it all

not a cleansing from but a return to her after all? I had protected my son from her, yet I had no defense - not when the
image of her magenta hair became the body summoning, im-
ploring me with the cover of indifference. The want unwanted for us both.

He heard his son turn over in his sleep. This journey is over
for now, I have not mourned and disengaged enough to go
through this night to the next sun. Then he was waking up
and in the next room he heard his son get up to go to the
bathroom, so he turned over and went back to sleep. The
next morning, he made both of them a breakfast heartier
than usual. Butter melting down the popovers and the bacon
grease consuming every other smell of the kitchen.

He fed the kitty and got his son's book bag in order. He
added two more sharpened pencils. He patted his son on the
back twice with encouragement in facing the challenges of
the day. Then he waited at the bus and waved goodbye to a
son fortunately already engaged with the other children.

He sat with his second cup of coffee and the image of the
magenta hair returned again, unsummoned and unwanted.
He was about to move away from it in a flight of sorts, but
then, noticing the time and its generous gap from when he
had to leave, he sat completely still. Let it come he thought,
give me what you've got, you haunting bitch.

I didn't mean that I thought once I heard it in my head. I'm sorry Sandy, I didn't mean that, but you were a mess and often mean. No, I'm not through with the rage of who you were. I saw her beckoning again as she had done during the night walk. What more do you want of me? I asked her. You've taken everything but him and, in some ways, you still have him too. You still have your dirty paws around his neck, at times you do, and don't think I don't know it.

I put my head in my hands. I howled internally. It was such a strange sound, as if a wolf was speaking in tongues, elevating the howl higher and higher in pitch as seemingly random syllables fell out. There seemed no sense to what was happening now as there had been no sense in any of my relationship with her. But I stayed with it, suddenly realizing that this in fact was the continuation of the night walk and it was past 2 am, moving forward to the next sun.

So, I went to the syllables and stayed with their flow, syllables rolling, yelling, crying and then successively catapulting then simply flowing: I knew intuitively such flow had to do with the water, with the Spirit of the water, that basic trust of the base of all things. Amniotic, sperm flowing to the moist womb, flow where all had become dry. Flow so what is sticky can disengage and move. Waters, waters with air in them, bubbling. The waters that come after the time of the Spirit with fire. This is not the water that had been there before the fire, this is the water coming after the fire, after the fire had burnt and there was only scorched earth and the pollutions all had been turned to ash.

He stayed for a while, head in hands and he felt her come and touch his head, run her hand down his hair. She no longer was beckoning but she was saying that he had gotten the message and she could leave.

On the way to work, he tapped on the steering wheel a tune that was repeating in his head. He wasn't aware of having known it before, but it was catchy and interesting. The downward cascade of the water was in it. He caught the cadence in his heart. He stepped out of his car into a slim mud puddle. Water in all sorts of places unnoticed before: the humidity of the air, the tears from these eyes as they hit the colder air outside the car, the moisture on the windowpane when he went to open it in his office, the smell of dampness as he watered the one living plant in the room.

He was at the coffeepot; a colleague was across the room arranging the documents. In many ways, her job was more challenging than his. He looked at her thin belt that was tinged a light silver. The money she brought into the company was remarkable. She didn't pause to reconsider and regret much. He was thinking that he wasn't sure whether he was drawn to her since she was a threat of sorts or whether he was mostly lonely.

The magenta hair was far away now. The tune of the morning ride was still with me but as background music, as if I were in a mall. I see that I can move back and forth from hearing it in the distant background and then up close where it gets between me and her, between me and the others overall. He rubbed the edge of his coffee cup to keep the dripping from spilling on the rug.

Time went that day, swallowed into the requirements of the job and the appointments: some tenuous in sensibility yet again some cogent and closed. Could he say the water was moving around and through him? Did he even pause to wonder such?

The lack in what I did and did not do this day occupied my mind like a disgruntled tenant the whole way home. Omissions and commissions assaulted me and where was, where is, the water in that?! Nothing but raw edges in my mind, serrated, dried bone edges. They all live like that at work even the woman with the silver belt. The silver hue had matched her watch strap, it had matched her earrings, but I'm sure that the inside of her mind is dry edges. Even the best of the women is lacking the water as is most every man I know. Call it holy, call it sacred or the Holy Spirit. It is the water in the

Samaritan Well, the ocean walked upon, even the blood in the chalice. Was it red this post-fire water?

I drove up and quickly changed my clothes and ran to the corner to pick up Marty from the bus. The magenta hair often came back at such a time but did not now. It may be that she finally did leave, I thought. I sneezed with a hardy release. It wasn't a goodbye for now or a good riddance but a thank you, I see what I need, what the next message is for well-being, for not succumbing to the transgressions.

For not doing the many transgressions that I have done. They were down the pike. Magenta was interwoven with them. I have repented, I have atoned though I know that sounds prideful. I do not know nor most likely will never know where she is with such atonement. She came with a message so she cannot be far from it but that is a wish. Was she lacking connection with the water? Aren't we all?

I made a simple dinner and my boy appreciated it. He was taking apart his toy robot to see how it was made. Do robots have brains, Daddy? No, not like we have brains. How do they know where to go and how to move then? They are programmed by humans. TV programs? No, like computer programs - information we put into them telling them how to work, and, by the way, do you want to go ice-skating tomorrow?

It was one of his favorite sports and he preferred it outside. At first, I would stand with the other parents and watch but the cold made headway with the inside of my bones. So, I took on skating with him though I knew he preferred to be with his friends, and, after a time, I would leave them and make the wide figure eights in a kind of meditative dance.

Water on the ice, not only in the ice, and I saw how our gestures, our positioning in motion also is of the water. I flowed more agilely and with less self-consciousness. The deep bending of my left shoulder was curving into the ice but never touching it. I almost fell twice yet that was of no consequence; I continued the bending, the slowing bent shoulder into the figuring eights.

The bystanders must have thought many things watching him, but he didn't care even when he noted their varied expressions looking towards him. He dipped widely again and again and then it was his son skating over to him. I have a pass for another Saturday Daddy - we can come for free; I won a raffle! His son was delighted, his son was eager and almost shaking with this delight in a way that was difficult to distinguish from agitation.

The excitement that buoys and tremors through us - he held his son closely to his chest challenging anyone there to look askance at such. He hugged him as if they were about to separate for a long trip. He kissed Marty's cheek. He took off the boy's skates and then he took off his own. He slung them over his back as if they were old timers at the pond instead of members of a formal ice rink indoors and at a cost.

The thought flashed across his mind that perhaps his son was to go with him, accompany him on the night walk past 2 am now towards the next sun. Now he knew they would have to be close to the water to do so, and that without such protection and guidance there would be the danger of catapulting into the sun, both burning ablaze, delicately strewn afterwards with neither identity nor insight ever possible.

But when we returned home, the old loneliness was waiting for us. My son had his robot, but I knew he had the loneliness also. We waited in this loneliness, and I knew he was not to accompany me further. Young developing bodies only can take so much I thought as he was sleeping, and I was on the walk in those woods at night again.

I thought of others who had taken night walks and I looked around for a guide; they all had had them. I checked my socks for any weapons I might have concealed without even knowing it. I didn't own literal weapons but looked for the invisible ones, the micro aggressions that come out through either tongue or computer key from the hurt, revengeful soul. I patted my belt area for any padding such as I had had in the past when I was Santa Claus to others in disguise in order to disguise my woe, inner torment, and failings.

I thought of those, particularly the main one with magenta, who had broken my heart, punctured it repetitively, slicing it slowly over time. As I maneuvered carefully over the stone and moss, I thought of any advantages that a cut through, cut open heart might have. There would be more opening perhaps for those also wounded. I smiled at this kind thought and wondered how the very night walk could lead to such benevolence.

He noted later that day, after the walk, when he was situated in the daily work environment, doing what he did everyday with slight slants of variation, that she had come back again during the walk of the last night, yet this time was there just for a moment and then it had gone right to a generous heart, a charitable thought. So, most likely it was over. He sighed in between meetings when this realization came to him.

Most likely it was over. He was at his desk, and he picked up an elastic band and stretched it repetitively. Rhythm. Water. His cut heart still beating, the waves of blood, loud surges of them finally cleansed - so was this night walk the final detox-ification? He reached for the next pile of registrations and proposals. His son's lunch flashed across his mind: had he put in enough carrots and celery?

He felt her presence before he saw her at his door. Yes, come in. It wasn't like she was asking, however, she had not disturbed the flow of her movement at his door to ask entry - he had just presumed that she would. Instead, she already had seeped in when he said the words come in. He might have said enter, but he was not that formal even at work. Neither the words enter nor come in seemed to be relevant to the scene since she just flowed through his door without stopping to ask. Yet it was not a hurried or contrived flow that could be a front for some sort of head-twist manipulation.

There she was. He had noticed her before but now, attuned to the water, he saw her. It was not that she would be the next mother of his son, but he knew, when he lifted his head still with elastic band between forefinger and thumb in a sort of wiggle itself, he knew she was significant.

I do not think I even know her name but there will be time to find out. For, unlike the silver belt woman and so many there, the sensibility within her movement without hidden agenda indicates that she was one of the few close to the water. I look up with a glance that must have been questioning her intent, her task into my official space.

She speaks her messages and her requests. I walk to the cabinet and get her the necessary paperwork. Her fingers have rings suggesting permanent linkages of her heart and mind. I don't care. This is not about our conjoining illicitly. I am on the night walk and there is no room for illicit. But being close to the water is really why she is here, why she is appearing before me.

What do I say? How does water and the knowledge that one has to be closer to it appear in daily discourse, the talk between colleagues? Stop thinking it through, I thought, just talk. So, I asked her how she was finding this last project. It's getting better as we begin to see the pattern within it all, she said, and our latest alterations really helped make it viable.

Who are you really? That is what I really wanted to ask. Why do you come now into my view during this time of the night walk? That is what I really wanted to ask.

Yet I knew the answer: it was because she was close to the water. As she departed from my office, I realized that I was afraid of her in a way. This was very different for me. Before, I would have been afraid of her because of her beauty or her mind. It wasn't that either of those were non-significant to me, but they did fall away in the process of the night walk. They got absorbed into the very stones upon which I walked there.

My fear of her resided somewhere else: it was in her very closeness to the water. So, I sat at my desk, in front of my computer, turned it off and wondered if it was the water I was afraid of or her being close to it. I saw how difficult it was to distinguish the two. My phone rang. At first, I thought it was my daughter, such a strange thought since I didn't have a daughter, yet that was the thought.

He spoke a few minutes with the manager of the company. It was about a favor that easily could be accomplished. He agreed to meet him at four o'clock in the conference room. He put his head in his hands and stroked his temples. More meetings were to come before four, he was required to be present, fully intelligent. She was at the meeting at three o'clock. When he entered the room, he nodded at her with a quickness that fit his fear. She smiled back while continuing the conversation in which she was engaging and seemingly enjoying.

He watched her gestures from a side glance and with a kinesthetic sense of her presence. Nothing of the business at hand and her responses to it suggested the water but it was in her open chest area. It was like a funnel moved out from her heart and lungs and stomach area and soothed the area around her so that those with her were calmed and sorted out. They sorted out their issues better, the issues known as they became more aware of those unknown. He could see the effect of her presence in the way one colleague apologized to one other: these two who usually were in demonstrable conflict. He could see this in the way he became more aware of hating a colleague who touched the competitive edge he had had with his father. Then he entered the work decisions with the rest, water or not there was work to do.

But what could be done without the water? Was there anything that can exist without it? He cleared his throat. He mentioned an official in the company who would be a big help with this project. The idea was taken up and a call was made. Then they called on her for the figures and projections. Her labor-intensive work was impressive and a help to the vision of where they could take the company in a five-year plan.

She left the meeting with a look in his direction almost as if they had exchanged a greeting at the start of it. He called to check in with his sitter who had picked up his son that day due to the 4 pm meeting. He went into the meeting tired but eager to find out the favor that the manager wanted from him, find out its requirement.

I had known Case for a time, and he never had wanted anything from me; we worked together side by side, he never took an upper stance with me though he was the manager. We all had stock in the company, we all wanted it to succeed and none of us really thought in terms of hierarchies in the working arrangement. I blew my nose. I sat near him at the conference table. I had no need of coffee but said I'd wait while he got some.

Case came back with it and a Danish. He was a tidy guy and always deliberate. I had liked him the minute I met him seven years ago. He was small in stature and bone structure, and his efficiency and clarity preceded him. He also was just a really nice guy which was more impressive since he had had some pretty harrowing losses.

Certainly, I said when he laid out what I could do for him. It would take not even four hours and I have the time, I told him with a soft slap on his shoulder. I saw his right hand rub the shine on the mahogany table. By his regard to what was not said yet meant, as well as his overall generosity to what wounds, I really thought that he was someone who knew the night walk also, but I wasn't sure he had made it all the way through. He would be different if he had. He wouldn't have that block of steel behind his forehead indicating he both knew the walk and often declined to partake in it.

I wanted to tell him that we could go together. I wanted to invite him without worrying whether his progress would be ahead or behind mine - I chuckled - as if that related at all to

the walk. He looked at me: Private joke? He asked. No, I said
slowly.

I thought then of the woman's funnel. I opened what was
there at my chest and stomach. Case looked at me. In that
look was the question asked and the answer given. Together
we would accompany one another on the night walk this
very evening.

The large solid granite at my right foot was shiny and I wondered about dew, and I wondered about slipping. But Case
was there, he just seemed to appear as soon as I began out
that night when my son was secure and sound asleep. I did
not see Case but felt him on my left. I was fairly sure that he
could not see me either. But the companionship made the
walk more possible. Yet where was our guide - others always
had them - where was the wise one from generations past or
the saint or the angel? But, of course, I knew they were here
and that is why Case could have found me.

Yet the humanity alongside me now made a difference. It
wasn't a question of safety as much as being with another
with a pulse. We could and would call on the guides when a
danger sensed by scent seemed to come yet the living pulse
beside me was necessary in a way, and the concreteness in
this necessity interested me.

They went slowly with arms outstretched and he thought of mountain goats. Goats on the mountainside over all sorts of crevices and slippery inclining slopes, yet surefooted and swift. He asked Case: Do you think we should pick up our pace? The manager now more friend shrugged and then agreed. Let's try it, he replied, I'm feeling steadier on these rocks.

How did you get here Case? I mean in the larger sense.

Can anyone really answer such a question? It's all in the Book, he smiled, and there was a hint of a chuckle.

But there are the choices. I almost stopped speaking. I could have stopped there, but then I added that it had to do with the water.

Water?

You didn't know?

No.

Then how can you be here?

The Book - way before I was a seed.

I see how you mean it now.

Water? He asked again.

I reached out to halt him. The terrain which had been rising was beginning a decline, short but definite.

Let's just say that the source of living, the fluidity within and connecting us all including future generations is within all and we are going to where there is a constant flow in which we can trust and from which we can learn but we're not there yet.

Right now, it's about this downward incline, Case said.

I almost slipped as he said it. He quickly reached for my arm to hold me up. Water is also slippery, he said.

Yes, it can be disengaging, I replied.

Together we crouched down to go on all fours frontward until the ground leveled. I thought I heard my son stirring, I looked at Case - could he hear it? What about his wife and children - could he hear them?

He looked back at me. He looked sad. Was it all too much for us - ought we go back to our familiar daily lives with their usual frustrations and triumphs?

No, I said to him as if he had asked the question - we are doing this for our kids. You see, we do have the choice - we both want on some level to sit down now and go back home. Do you want to do that now Case? Where are you?

I admit that I'm between here and there.

You see the choice part.

I do. I can frame it any way I want as completely determined but I know I can be back in bed with my wife any minute I decide to be. And I see that what I will choose is already in the Book. But yes, it is a choice.

Right. So, what is it then?

To go on - of course.

It's for them you know.

Primarily for them, he said.

Two more inclines followed by sharp declines that they navigated with their backs parallel to ground, face to sky, on all fours, quickly yet with an assurance that seemed strange to both. Time to call on the Holy Spirit? Case asked, clearly out of breath, and with an assurance that such existed as surely as those rocks.

I did that a while ago, I answered.

Is it on the right or the left?

The right shoulder.

Sometimes it seems to be in front of me, facing me.

Go with it, ask for help, direction.

Says slow down but keep going.

Some time elapsed before Case said: Well? I'm getting tired.

I heard that there's a house ahead.

And there it was. Quite modern looking. They knocked twice. An elderly lady answered. She looked like she could have been in the gingerbread house fairy tale. She even had a small, round lace cap on her head and a matching lace lined apron.

Young men? She said, slowly yet not distantly or with a sense that she had been rudely interrupted.

It's hard to explain what we need, I began, and we're on a night walk that facilitates knowing the water better.

Come in, she said with a smile yet more seriously than she had been in her greeting.

The rooms were also furnished with modern style furniture. No fairy tale gingerbread home here or any fairy tale home. Sharp edged designs and a spaciousness in the rooms. But still he felt, as did Case in the look they exchanged, that it was all surreal.

How can it be so modern here?

We are not divorced from your world, she said, we want to bring in the knowledge. Pioneers always think the terrain modern, very different but modern, that is, of their time.

No, this was no fairy tale grandmother.

She showed them the rooms as if the house was for sale and they were interested buyers.

At one point, Case sat on one of the chairs in the living room and put his head between his hands. The lady went to make us tea.

Case? I asked.

I'm afraid we'll never get back.

Holy Spirit was all I said.

Yes - I go to it and I see compassion on its face.

Returning, the lady said: It doesn't have gender, but sometimes it helps us to see it that way.

I see it, Case replied.

I'm not sure, maybe a daughter, I said.

The lady said: Ask what next.

The answer came swiftly to Case: To go see the rooms.

So, let's continue our tour, she said as she moved us into a room that looked like a den, a smaller room with cozier furniture, softer, more engaging, a sofa and two chairs with a TV.

Then we went into a spacious room with a large bed and sky light - the master bedroom presumably. It had a huge wall-size window on one side and when we looked there, we saw a river rushing by with a small waterfall plunging over shiny sun-lit rocks. It almost looked red in places, this river.

We both were aghast. There it was.

Is this place for sale? It was the first thing that came to my mind, so I said it without caution or censure or even checking with my friend.

$325,000, she said. Very fair.

Yes, yes, we both were nodding.

We continued the tour. The river didn't seem to be seen in the other rooms but now we heard it and felt it as if it was moving through every room and ourselves.

Do we bring our families here? Case asked me in a tentative tone.

What would that be - I thought out loud - living in a parallel universe to our daily one or leaving that one to only live in this?

Where is the guide? He was asking the lady now.

Empty your minds, it's there.

There were nowhere those words could have come from but the real estate lady - and so we both simultaneously turned around and she was still there in the room with us. Empty your minds, she said it again.

We paused. We sat. There was too much in these very minds to empty them. In fact, they seemed to fill up the more we tried the emptying. We opened our eyes which had been on and off shut and looked at her. She put out her left arm straight towards the window. We realized she was indicating the river. So, we went there, listening to its cadence, and, in a sense, inquiring what it wanted of us. Hearing it. There came the emptiness. There came the Holy Spirit and we continued to sit. I found myself putting my right hand to my heart, holding it there. Case opened his eyes after a time and then imitated me. To what might we be pledging allegiance? I asked him more seriously than I originally had intended.

Then I lay down, my arms by my side. Case was no longer there, nor the real estate lady, just the home and the river. I lay listening for a long time. Then I heard, very distinctly over it, my son stir.

I found myself walking into his bedroom, back in daily reality. He was waking up. I saw he had been sweating and I grabbed a tissue and began wiping his neck. These souls we spend our lives with and for whom we care so much. Would he, my Marty, ever go to the home at the end of the night-walk? Was I ever to return there?

The obvious questions to Case the next day did not get asked until mid-afternoon since there was so much to do with a complicated agenda that day. I stood there in his office, he did look rather dazed behind his desk, like a schoolboy with somewhat incomprehensible assignments. Yet of course I knew what really was incomprehensible to us both.

Where did you go while we were lying there? My question to him was out in this mid-afternoon. I turned and you were gone. Later I heard my son stir and I was walking into his room in pajamas as if I had been the entire night there in bed.

Same here. He looked up past me with an inquisitive look in his eyes and all over his face. He continued: I turned, and you were gone, and my wife was waking up and I was there awake beside her as if I never had left.

Do we need, I said, sitting in a leather uncomfortable chair there, do we need to discuss this with anyone - or just one another? I knew you could do it, go there with me. I knew you capable for the walk somehow. But now what? It makes it easier, more sensible somehow, the whole thing, because you were there, but it also makes it more "real" strangely enough.

Real Estate.

Real Estate lady.

Real Estate - that is, where or who we each *are* really.

$325?

I'm not sure.

What could money be in that place?

Effort?

For what?

To be of the water, the post-fire water, after we've been scorched, as you and I have been and done in our lives, the water after that. After the thoroughly being burnt and burning.

So many losses to get there - as if it's an accomplishment, he responded laughing.

But it's time, yes, the losses you and I each have had are extreme and maybe it's through that that I sensed you were on the night-walk.

Well, many are there then, he said, since life is getting more harrowing each day for so many.

Yes, but do they know it? And do they know it's about getting to the water?

By now they were leaving the office. Where to go to discuss such things? They stood by each of their cars and then he signaled for Case to follow him.

He found himself leading his friend into a cathedral. They both were unfamiliar with this one, but it was gorgeous and struck all their senses bringing a kind of relief. This is where we meditate and pray, yes pray, on the water, what being of the water is.

Water - Reflection.

So, that is how specifics in the outer world always are reflecting to each of us what needs to dislodge more internally, be understood, grappled with, and sorted through.

Water - Flow.

Rocks are not prohibitive but part of it. In essence, the flow, the river is where rocks, seemingly concrete blockages, can be part of the direction and movement without losing their reality or substance but being useful to the river in terms of how and where to proceed to enhance the flow.

Water - Splash - Bubbles.

Air in water. The water has cognitive momentum as well. Airy, ethereal, of Spirit. What we all have to know. Angels bursting out of it, sparks of air and light. Air and fire and earth all there within it.

Fluids in our body. Urine. Phlegm. Semen and Uterine fluids. Tears. Sweat. Blood. Where the water is in us and wants attention.

It's our will that blocks it as we try to protect ourselves. Afraid of the water since it is moving in its own direction.

And what comes up against it is our blocks, dysfunctions, in our life and those who came before us and generated us.

So, it's not that we have to undo or remove the rocks?

No - they're our identity, heritage, and environments. But if they become a dam, if we make them a dam, then problems.

They become a dam when we harden which is when we retaliate. When the invasions and betrayals that attack our entrails are not processed, digested, and so we harden and retaliate often destructively. Sin as deadwood blocking the water's flow.

The two sat silently in this meditation, speaking silently about the relation of blocks and dysfunctions to sin and how the night walk was part of going through such to the clarity of messages.

Then they went home to their families, but they never left the cathedral or the 325 home. They went into buying the home together as half-and-half owners. They brought there the deepest wounds of the entrails, at times with one another present and at times alone.

Did they ever ask the source of the river you may ask?

No, but they had faith in that. They knew it was beyond them and had an intelligence beyond theirs. Since they had this new other home, they were able to follow what they had never noticed before but were signposts - indicating which way to turn, what to say, what to hold back and what to give out.

Signposts? you ask.

Like the dream that allowed the Magi to not return to Herod, like the writing in the sand, like the sun hiding its rays.

Water rushes, water rushes through them, and each experiences the being entered, a cleansing, coursing through circuit, and then they saw her, and she was not only angel or muse or wane moon wise. She was all of them and the culmination into what next.

Connected to their real estate, below head and heart, and yet fed by both instead of lead by both or either which is why they couldn't see such signposts before. Asking, supplicating as they learned in the 325 home, and letting the holy water clean out the entrails and flow through head and heart down to intestines and up to settle in stomach where the digestion can be complete.